TWO LITTLE WOMEN
ON A HOLIDAY

"It would make a fine lavamere," said Dolly, holding it up against her chest, and glancing in a nearby mirror. (*Page* 163)

TWO LITTLE WOMEN
ON A HOLIDAY

BY

CAROLYN WELLS

AUTHOR OF

**THE PATTY BOOKS, THE MARJORIE BOOKS,
TWO LITTLE WOMEN SERIES, ETC.**

FRONTISPIECE BY

E. C. CASWELL

GROSSET & DUNLAP
PUBLISHERS   NEW YORK

CONTENTS

TWO LITTLE WOMEN
ON A HOLIDAY

TWO LITTLE WOMEN ON A HOLIDAY

CHAPTER I

A WONDERFUL PLAN

"HELLO, Dolly," said Dotty Rose, over the telephone.

"Hello, Dot," responded Dolly Fayre. "What
you want?"

"Oh! I can't tell you this way. Come on over,
just as quick as you can."

"But I haven't finished my Algebra, and it's
nearly dinner time, anyway."

"No it isn't,— and no matter if it is. Come on, I
tell you! You'd come fast enough if you knew what
it's about!"

"Tell me, then."

"I say I can't,— over the telephone. Oh, Dolly,
come on, and stop fussing!"

The telephone receiver at Dotty's end of the wire

was hung up with a click, and Dolly began to waggle her receiver hook in hope of getting Dotty back. But there was no response, so Dolly rose and went for her coat. Flinging it round her, and not stopping to get a hat, she ran next door to Dotty Rose's house.

It was mid January, and the six o'clock darkness was lighted only by the street lights. Flying across the two lawns that divided the houses, Dolly found Dotty awaiting her at the side door.

"Hurry up in, Doll," she cried, eagerly, "the greatest thing you ever heard! Oh, the very greatest! If you only *can!* Oh, if you *only* can!"

"Can what? Do tell me what you're talking about." Dolly tossed her coat on the hall rack, and followed Dotty into the Roses' living-room. There she found Dotty's parents and also Bernice Forbes and her father. What could such a gathering mean? Dolly began to think of school happenings; had she cut up any mischievous pranks or inadvertently done anything wrong? What else could bring Mr. Forbes to the Roses' on what was very evidently an important errand? For all present were eagerly interested,— that much was clear. Mr. and Mrs. Rose were smiling, yet shaking their heads in uncertainty; Bernice was flushed and excited; and Mr. Forbes himself was apparently trying to persuade them to something he was proposing.

This much Dolly gathered before she heard a word of the discussion. Then Mrs. Rose said, " Here's Dolly Fayre. You tell her about it, Mr. Forbes."

" Oh, let me tell her," cried Bernice.

" No," said Mr. Rose, " let her hear it first from your father. You girls can chatter afterward."

So Mr. Forbes spoke. " My dear child," he said to Dolly, " my Bernice is invited to spend a week with her uncle, in New York City. She is privileged to ask you two girls to accompany her if you care to."

Dolly listened, without quite grasping the idea. She was slow of thought, though far from stupid. And this was such a sudden and startling suggestion that she couldn't quite take it in.

" Go to New York, for a week. Oh, I couldn't. I have to go to school."

Mrs. Rose smiled. " That's just the trouble, Dolly. Dot has to go to school, too,— at least, she ought to. Bernice, likewise. But this invitation is so delightful and so unusual, that I'm thinking you three girls ought to take advantage of it. The question is, what will your parents say?"

"Oh, they'll never let me go!" exclaimed Dolly, decidedly. "They don't want anything to interfere with my lessons."

"No, and we feel the same way about Dotty. But an exceptional case must be considered in an exceptional manner. I think your people might be persuaded if we go about it in the right way."

"I don't believe so," and Dolly looked very dubious. "Tell me more about it."

"Oh, Doll, it's just gorgeous!" broke in Bernice. "Uncle Jeff,— he's father's brother,— wants me to spend a week with him. And he's going to have my cousin, Alicia, there at the same time. And he wants us to bring two other girls, and Alicia can't bring one, 'cause she's at boarding school, and none of the girls can get leave,— that is, none that she wants. So Uncle said for me to get two, if I could,— and I want you and Dot."

"A whole week in New York! Visiting!" Dolly's eyes sparkled as the truth began to dawn on her. "Oh, I *wish* I could coax Mother into it. I've never been to New York to stay any time. Only just for the day. How lovely of you, Bernie, to ask us!"

"There's no one else I'd rather have, but if you can't go, I'll have to ask Maisie May. I must get two."

"Are you going anyway, Dots?"

"I don't know. I want to go terribly, but I don't want to go without you, Dolly. Oh, *won't* your mother let you?"

"The only way to find out is to ask her," said Mr. Forbes, smiling. "Suppose I go over there now and ask. Shall I go alone, or take you three chatter-boxes along?"

"Oh, let us go," and Dotty sprang up; "we can coax and you can tell about the arrangements."

"Very well," agreed Mr. Forbes, "come along, then."

So the four went across to the Fayre house, and found the rest of Dolly's family gathered in the library.

"Here is Mr. Forbes, Daddy," said Dolly, as they entered.

Mr. and Mrs. Fayre and Trudy, Dolly's older sister, greeted the visitor cordially, and looked with smiling inquiry at the eager faces of the three girls.

Dolly went and sat on the arm of her mother's chair, and, putting an arm around her, whispered, "Oh, Mumsie, please, *please* do say yes! Oh, please do!"

"Yes to what?" returned Mrs. Fayre, patting her daughter's shoulder.

"Mr. Forbes will tell you. Listen."

"It's this way, my dear people," began Mr. Forbes. He was a man with an impressive manner, and it seemed as if he were about to make a speech of grave importance, as, indeed, from the girls' point of view, he was. "My brother Jefferson, who lives in New York, has invited my daughter to spend a week in his home there. He has asked also another niece, Miss Alicia Steele. He wants these girl visitors to bring with them two friends, and as Alicia does not wish to avail herself of that privilege, Bernice may take two with her. She wants to take Dotty and Dolly. There, that's the whole story in a nutshell. The question is, may Dolly go?"

"When is this visit to be made?" asked Mrs. Fayre.

"As soon as convenient for all concerned. My

brother would like the girls to come some day next week, and remain one week."

"What about school?" and Mrs. Fayre looked decidedly disapproving of the plan.

"That's just it!" exclaimed Dotty. "We knew you'd say that! But, Mrs. Fayre, my mother says this is the chance of a lifetime,— almost,— and we ought, we really *ought* to take advantage of it."

"But to be out of school for a whole week,— and what with getting ready and getting home and settled again, it would mean more than a week —"

"But, mother, we could make up our lessons," pleaded Dolly, "and I *do* want to go! oh, I do want to go, just *awfully!*"

"I should think you would," put in Trudy. "Let her go, mother, it'll be an education in itself, — the visit will. Why, the girls can go to the museums and art galleries and see all sorts of things."

"Of course we can," said Bernice, "and my uncle has a beautiful house and motor cars and everything!"

"That's another point," said Mr. Fayre, gravely.

"You must realise, Mr. Forbes, that my little girl is not accustomed to grandeur and wealth. I don't want her to enjoy it so much that she will come back discontented with her own plain home."

"Oh, nonsense, my dear sir! A glimpse of city life and a taste of frivolity will do your girl good. Dolly is too sensible a sort to be a prey to envy or discontent. I know Dolly fairly well, and I can vouch for her common sense!"

"So can I," said Bernice. "Doll will enjoy everything to the limit, but it won't hurt her disposition or upset her happiness to see the sights of the city for a short time. Oh, please, Mr. Fayre, do let her go."

"Just as her mother thinks," and Mr. Fayre smiled at the insistent Bernice.

"Tell me of the household," said Mrs. Fayre. "Is your brother's wife living?"

"Jeff has never been married," replied Mr. Forbes. "He is an elderly bachelor, and, I think is a bit lonely, now and then. But he is also a little eccentric. He desires no company, usually. It is most extraordinary that he should ask these girls. But I think he wants to see his two nieces, and he fears he cannot entertain them pleasantly unless they have other companions of their own age."

" And who would look after the girls? "

" Mrs. Berry, my brother's housekeeper. She is a fine noble-hearted and competent woman, who has kept his house for years. I know her, and I am perfectly willing to trust Bernice to her care. She will chaperon the young people, for I doubt if my brother will go to many places with them. But he will want them to have the best possible time, and will give them all the pleasure possible."

" That part of it is all right, then," smiled Mrs. Fayre; " it is, to my mind, only the loss of more than a week of the school work that presents the insuperable objection."

" Oh, don't say insuperable," urged Mr. Forbes. " Can't you bring yourself to permit that loss? As Dolly says, the girls can make up their lessons."

" They can — but will they? "

" I will, mother," cried Dolly; " I promise you I will study each day while I'm in New York. Then I can recite out of school hours after I get back, and I'll get my marks all the same."

" But, Dolly dear, you can't study while you are

in New York. There would be too much to distract you and occupy your time."

"Oh, no, Mrs. Fayre," observed Bernice, " we couldn't be all the time sightseeing. I think it would be fine for all us girls to study every day, and keep up our lessons that way."

"It sounds well, my dear child," and Mrs. Fayre looked doubtfully at Bernice, " and I daresay you mean to do it, but I can't think you could keep it up. The very spirit of your life there would be all against study."

"I agree with that," said Mr. Forbes, decidedly. " I vote for the girls having an entire holiday. Lessons each day would spoil all their fun."

"They couldn't do it," Trudy said. "I know, however much they tried, they just *couldn't* study in that atmosphere."

"Why not?" asked Bernice. "We're not young ladies, like you, Trudy. We won't be going to parties, and such things. We can only go to the shops and the exhibitions and for motor rides in the park and such things. We could study evenings, I'm sure."

"It isn't only the lessons," Mrs. Fayre said; " but

I can't feel quite willing to let my little girl go away for a week without me." Her pleasant smile at Mr. Forbes robbed the words of any reflection they might seem to cast on his brother's invitation. " I'm sure Mrs. Berry would do all that is necessary in the way of a chaperon's duties, but these girls are pretty young even for that. They need a parent's over-sight."

Mrs. Fayre was about to say a mother's over-sight, when she remembered that Bernice had no mother, and changed the words accordingly.

There was some further discussion, and then Mrs. Fayre said she must have a little time alone to make up her mind. She knew that if Dolly did not go, Maisie May would be asked in her place, but she still felt undecided. She asked for only an hour or two to think it over, and promised to telephone di-rectly after dinner, and tell Mr. Forbes her final decision. This was the only concession she would make. If not acceptable then her answer must be no.

" Please do not judge my wife too harshly," said Mr. Fayre as he accompanied Mr. Forbes and Bernice to the door. " She still looks upon Dolly as her baby, and scarcely lets her out of her sight."

"That's all right," returned Mr. Forbes. "She's the right sort of a mother for the girl. I hope she will decide to let Dolly go, but if not, I quite understand her hesitancy, and I respect and admire her for it. Bernice can take somebody else, and I trust you will not try over hard to influence Mrs. Fayre in Dolly's favour. If anything untoward should happen, I should never forgive myself. I would far rather the children were disappointed than to have Mrs. Fayre persuaded against her better judgment."

The Forbeses departed, and then Dotty Rose went home, too.

"Oh, Dollyrinda," she whispered as they stood in the hall, "do you s'pose your mother'll *ever* say yes?"

"I don't believe so," replied Dolly mournfully. "But, oh, Dot, how I do want to go! Seems 'sif I never wanted anything so much in all my life!"

"You don't want to go a bit more than I want to have you. Why, Dollops, I shan't go, if you don't."

"Oh, yes, you will, Dotty. You must. It would be silly not to."

"But I couldn't! I just *couldn't*. Do you s'pose I could have one single bit of fun going to places without you? And knowing you were here at home, longing to be with us! No-sir-ee! I just couldn't pos-*sib*-ly! So just you remember that, old girl; no Dolly,— no Dotty! And that's *sure!*"

There was a ring in Dotty's voice that proclaimed an unshakable determination, and Dolly knew it. She knew that no coaxing of Bernice or even of Dolly herself, could make Dotty go without her chum.

For chums these two were, in the deepest sense of the word. They were together all that was possible during their waking hours. They studied together, worked and played together, and occupied together their little house, built for them, and called Treasure House.

Dolly knew she couldn't enjoy going anywhere without Dotty, and she knew Dot felt the same way about her. But this was such a big, splendid opportunity, that she hated to have Dotty miss it, even if she couldn't go herself. The two girls said goodnight, and Dolly went back to her family in the library.

"I hate terribly to disappoint you, Dolly darling,"

began her mother, and the tears welled up in Dolly's blue eyes. This beginning meant a negative decision, that was self evident, but Dolly Fayre was plucky by nature and she was not the sort that whines at disappointment.

"All right," she said, striving to be cheerful, and blinking her eyes quickly to keep those tears back.

"Now, look here, Edith," said Mr. Fayre, "I don't believe I can stand this. I don't differ with you regarding the children, but I do think you might let Dolly go on this party. Even if it does take a week out of school, she'll get enough general information and experience from a week in the city to make up."

"That's just it, Will. But the experiences she gets there may not be the best possible for a little girl of fifteen."

"Oh, fifteen isn't an absolute baby. Remember, dear, Dolly is going to grow up some day, and she's getting started."

"And another thing. I asked Mr. Forbes a few questions while you were talking to Bernice, and it seems this other girl, the niece, Alicia, is attending a very fashionable girls' boarding school."

"Well, what of that? You speak as if she were attending a lunatic asylum!"

"No; but can't you see if Dolly goes to stay a week with wealthy Bernice Forbes and this fashionable Alicia, she'll get her head full of all sorts of notions that don't belong there?"

"No, I won't, mother," murmured Dolly, who, again on her mother's arm chair, was looking earnestly into the maternal blue eyes, so like her own. And very lovingly Mrs. Fayre returned the gaze, for she adored her little daughter and was actuated only by the best motives in making her decisions.

"And, here's another thing," said Dolly, "Dot won't go, if I don't. It seems too bad to spoil *her* fun."

"Oh, yes, she will," said Mrs. Fayre, smiling. "She would be foolish to give up her pleasure just because you can't share it."

"Foolish or not, she won't go," repeated Dolly. "I know my Dot, and when she says she won't do a thing, she just simply doesn't do it!"

"I'd be sorry to be the means of keeping Dotty at home," and Mrs. Fayre sighed deeply.

CHAPTER II

ALL through dinner time, Mrs. Fayre was some-what silent, her eyes resting on Dolly with a wistful, uncertain expression. She wanted to give the child the pleasure she craved, but she had hard work to bring herself to the point of overcoming her own objections.

At last, however, when the meal was nearly over, she smiled at her little daughter, and said, " All right, Dolly, you may go."

" Oh, mother! " Dolly cried, overwhelmed with sudden delight. " Really? Oh, I am so glad! Are you sure you're willing? "

" I've persuaded myself to be willing, against my will," returned Mrs. Fayre, whimsically. " I confess I just hate to have you go, but I can't bear to deprive you of the pleasure trip. And, as you say, it would also keep Dotty at home, and so, altogether, I think I shall have to give in."

"Oh, you angel mother! You blessed lady! How good you are!" And Dolly flew around the table and gave her mother a hug that nearly suffocated her.

"There, there, Dollygirl," said her father, "go back and finish your pudding while we talk this over a bit. Are you sure, Edith, you are willing? I don't want you to feel miserable and anxious all the week Dolly is cut loose from your apron string."

"No, Will; it's all right. If you and the Roses and Trudy, here, all agree it's best for Dolly to go, it seems foolish for me to object. And it may be for her good, after all."

"That's what I say, mother," put in Trudy. "Doll isn't a child, exactly. She's fifteen and a half, and it will be a fine experience for her to see a little bit of the great world. And she couldn't do it under better conditions than at Mr. Forbes' brother's. The Forbes' are a fine family, and you know, perfectly well, there'll be nothing there that isn't just exactly right."

"It isn't that, Trudy. But,— oh, I don't know; I daresay I'm a foolish mother bird, afraid of her littlest fledgling."

"You're a lovely mother-bird!" cried Dolly, "and not foolish a bit! but, oh, do decide positively, for I can't wait another minute to tell Dot, if I'm going."

"Very well," said Mrs. Fayre, "run along and tell Dotty, and Bernice, too."

Dolly made a jump and two hops for the telephone, and soon the wires must have bent under the weight of joyous exclamations.

"Oh, Dolly, isn't it fine!"

"Oh, Dotty, it's splendid! I can hardly believe it!"

"Have you told Bernice?"

"Not yet. Had to tell you first. When do we go?"

"Next Tuesday, I think. Now, you tell Bernie, so she can write to her uncle that we accept."

And then there was another jubilation over the telephone.

"Fine!" cried Bernice, as she heard the news. "Lovely! I'd so much rather have you two girls than any others. I'll write Uncle Jeff to-night that I'll bring you. And I'll come over to-morrow, and we'll decide what clothes to take, and all that."

Mrs. Fayre sighed, as Dolly reported this conversation.

"You girls can't do a bit of serious study all the rest of the time before you go," she said. "Now, Dolly, I'll have to ask you to do your lessons every day, before you plan or talk over the trip at all."

"Yes, mother, I will," and Dolly started at once for her schoolbooks.

It was hard work to put her mind on her studies, with the wonderful possibilities that lay ahead of her. But she was exceedingly conscientious, was Dolly Fayre, and she resolutely put the subject of the New York visit out of her mind, and did her algebra examples with diligence.

Not so, Dotty Rose. After Dolly's telephone message, she flung her schoolbooks aside, with a shout of joy, and declared she couldn't study that night.

"I don't wonder," laughed her father. "Why, Dot, you're going on a veritable Fairy-tale visit. You are quite justified in being excited over it."

"I thought you and Dolly didn't like Bernice Forbes very much," said Mrs. Rose.

"We didn't use to, mother. But lately, she's

been a whole lot nicer. You know Doll made her sort of popular, and after that, she helped along, herself, by being ever so much more pleasant and chummy with us all. She used to be stuck up and disagreeable; ostentatious about being rich, and all that. But nowadays, she's more simple, and more agreeable every way."

"That's nice," observed Mr. Rose. "Forbes is not a popular man, nor a very good citizen; I mean he isn't public-spirited or generous. But he's a fine business man and a man of sound judgment and integrity. I'm glad you're chums with his daughter, Dotty. And you ought to have a perfectly gorgeous time on the New York visit."

"Oh, we will, Daddy; I'm sure of that. What about clothes, Mumsie?"

"I'll have to see about that. You'll need a few new frocks, I suppose, but we can get them ready made, or get Miss Felton to come for a few days. There's nearly a week before you start."

"I want some nice things," declared Dotty. "You know Bernice has wonderful clothes, and I suppose her cousin has, too."

"Maybe your wardrobe can't be as fine as a rich

man's daughter," said her father smiling at her, " but I hope mother will fix you up so you won't feel ashamed of your clothes."

" I think they'll be all right," and Mrs. Rose nodded her head. " I'll see Mrs. Fayre to-morrow, and we'll find out what Bernice is going to take with her. You children can't need elaborate things, but they must be right."

The Rose family spent the entire evening talking over the coming trip, and when Dotty went to bed she set an alarm clock, that she might rise early in the morning to do her lessons for the day before breakfast. She did them, too, and came to the table, smiling in triumph.

" Did all my examples and learned my history perfectly," she exulted. " So you see, mother, my trip won't interfere with my education! "

" Oh, you can make up your lessons," said her father, carelessly. " I wouldn't give much for a girl who couldn't do a few extra tasks to make up for a grand outing such as you're to have."

" I either! " agreed Dotty. " But the Fayres are worried to death for fear Doll will miss a lesson somewhere."

"Dolly learns more slowly than you," remarked her mother. "You have a gift for grasping facts quickly, and a good memory to retain them."

"You ought to be grateful for that," said Mr. Rose.

"I am," returned Dotty. "When I see Dolly grubbing over her history, I can't understand how she can be so long over it."

"But she's better in mathematics than you are."

"Yes, she is. She helps me a lot with the old puzzlers. She thinks we'll study in New York. But somehow, I don't believe we will."

"Of course, you won't," laughed Mr. Rose. "Why, you'd be foolish to do that. A fine opportunity has come to you girls, and I advise you to make the most of it. See all the sights you can; go to all the pleasant places you can; and have all the fun you can cram into your days. Then go to sleep and rest up for the next day."

"Good, sound advice, Dads," said Dotty; "you're a gentleman and a scholar to look at it like that! But I don't know as we can go about much; I believe Mr. Forbes is quite an old man, and who will take us about?"

"I thought the housekeeper would," said Mrs. Rose.

"I don't know at all, mother. It seems Bernie has never visited there before, though she has been to the house. Her uncle is queer, and why he wants his two nieces all of a sudden, and his two nieces' friends, nobody knows. It's sort of mysterious, I think."

"Well, it's all right, as long as you're properly invited. It seems strange Bernie's cousin didn't care to take a friend."

"Yes; I wonder what she's like. Bernice hasn't seen her since they were little girls. She lives out in Iowa, I think. She's at school in Connecticut somewhere. It's all sort of unknown. But I like that part of it. I love new experiences."

"I always do too, Dot," said her father. "I reckon when you come home, you'll have lots to tell us."

"New York isn't so strange to me," said Dotty. "I've been there a lot of times, you know. But to go and stay in a house there,— that's the fun. It's so different from going in for a day's shopping with mother. Or the day we all went to the Hippodrome."

"You'll probably go to the Hippodrome again, or some such entertainment," suggested Mrs. Rose.

"I dunno. I imagine the old gentleman doesn't favour such gaiety. And the housekeeper lady will likely be too busy to do much for us. We can't go anywhere alone, can we?"

"I don't know," replied Mrs. Rose. "You must be guided by circumstances, Dotty. Whatever Mr. Forbes and Mrs. Berry say for you to do, will be all right. Make as little trouble as you can, and do as you're told. You'll have fun enough, just being with the girls."

"Indeed I will! Oh, I'm so glad Dolly can go! I wouldn't have stirred a step without her!"

"No, I know you wouldn't," agreed her mother.

Next day at school recess, Bernice showed the girls a letter she had received from Alicia.

"You know I haven't seen her in years," Bernice said; "I think she must be more grown up than we are, though she's only just sixteen."

"*Dearest Bernice:*" the letter ran.

"Isn't it simply screaming that we're to camp out at Uncle Jeff's! I'm wildly excited over it! Do you know why he has asked us? I'm not sure, my-

-❬ 24 ❭-

self, but I know there's a reason, and it's a secret.
I heard aunt and father talking about it when I was
home at Christmas time, but when I drifted into the
room, they shut up like clams. However, we'll have
one gay old time! Think of being in New York a
whole week! I don't want to take any of the girls
from here, for fear they'd bring back tales. Don't
you bring anybody you can't trust. Oh, I've laid
lots of plans, but I won't tell you about them till I
see you. Bring all your best clothes, and ask your
father for quite a lot of money, though I suppose
Uncle Jeff will give us some. I can scarcely wait for
the time to come!

> "Devotedly yours,
>> "ALICIA."

"What does she mean by a secret reason for your
going?" asked Dolly.

"I haven't an idea," replied Bernice. "My father
knows, though, I'm quite sure, 'cause he smiled at
that part of Alicia's letter. But he wouldn't tell me.
He only said, 'Oh, pshaw, nothing of any consequence. It's very natural that a lonely old bachelor
uncle should want to see his little girl nieces, and it's
very kind and thoughtful of him to ask you to bring
friends.' He says Uncle Jeff is not fond of company,

and spends all his time by himself. He's a scientist
or naturalist or something, and works in his study
all day. So, dad says, it'll be fine for us girls to
have four of us to be company for each other."

"It's gorgeous!" sighed Dotty, in an ecstasy of
anticipation. "But what does your cousin mean by
bringing a lot of money? We can't do that,— and
our parents don't let us spend much money ourselves,
anyway."

"Oh, that'll be all right," said Bernice, carelessly.
"We won't need much money. And if we go to
matinées, or anything like that, of course, I'll pay,
if Uncle Jeff doesn't. You two girls are my guests,
you know. You needn't take any money at all."

"All right," said Dolly, and dismissed the subject.
Money did not figure very largely in her affairs, as,
except for a small allowance for trifles, she never
handled any. Nor did Dotty, as these two were still
looked upon as children by their parents.

But motherless Bernice bought her own clothes and
paid her own bills; and so generous was her father,
that there was no stint, and as a consequence, she
too, cared and thought little about money as a con-
sideration.

"I'm a little scared of that Alicia person," said Dolly to Dotty as they walked home from school.

"Pooh! I'm not. She's no richer than Bernie."

"It isn't that. I'm not afraid of rich people. But she seems so grown up and — well, experienced."

"Well, sixteen is grown up. And we're getting there, Dolly. I shall put up my hair while I'm in New York."

"Why, Dot Rose! Really?"

"Yes, that is if Alicia does. Bernice often does, you know."

"I know it. I'll ask mother if I may."

"Goodness, Dolly, can't you decide a thing like that for yourself? What would your mother care?"

"I'd rather ask her," returned the conscientious Dolly.

Mrs. Fayre smiled when Dolly put the question. "I've been expecting that," she said. "You'd better do as the others do, dear. If they twist up their pigtails, you do the same."

"I'll show you how," offered Trudy. "If you're going to do it, you may as well learn a becoming fashion."

So Trudy taught her little sister how to coil up her yellow, curly mop in a correct fashion, and very becoming it was to Dolly.

But it made her look a year or two older than she was.

"Oh!" exclaimed her mother, when she saw her. "Where's my baby? I've lost my little girl!"

"Just as well," said Dolly, delighted at her achievement and pirouetting before a mirror. "It's time I began to be a little grown up, mother."

"Yes, I suppose it is. I felt just the same when Trudy put up her curls for the first time. I am a foolish old thing!"

"Now, don't you talk like that," cried Dolly, "or I'll pull down my hair and wear it in tails till I'm fifty!"

"No, dear; do as you like about it. And, if you want to wear it that way while you're in New York. do. It's all right."

More discussions came with the new dresses. Mrs. Fayre was for keeping to the more youthful models, but Mrs. Rose felt that the girls should have slightly older styles. Bernice's frocks were almost young ladyish, but those were not copied.

Dotty and Dolly always had their things similar, different in colouring but alike in style. So their respective mothers had many confabs before the grave questions were settled.

And the result was two very attractive wardrobes that were really right for fifteen-year-old girls. Afternoon dresses of voile or thin silk, and one pretty party dress for each of dainty chiffon and lace. Morning frocks of linen and a tailored street suit seemed to be ample in amount and variety.

Bernice had more and grander ones, but the two D's were entirely satisfied, and watched the packing of their small trunks with joyful contentment.

Dolly put in her diary, declaring she should write a full account of each day's happenings.

"Then that'll do for me," said Dotty. "I hate to keep a diary, and what would be the use? It would be exactly like yours, Doll, and I can borrow yours to read to my people after you've read it to your family."

"All right," agreed Dolly, good-naturedly, for what pleased one girl usually suited the other.

They didn't take their schoolbooks, for it made a heavy load, and too, all agreed that it would spoil the pleasant vacation. The girls promised to make up the lessons on their return, and so it seemed as if nothing marred the anticipation of their splendid holiday.

CHAPTER III

THE ARRIVAL

THE girls were put on the train at Berwick and as Mrs. Berry was to meet them at the station in New York, they were allowed to make the trip alone.

"I think this train ride the best part of the whole thing," said Dolly, as she took off her coat and hung it up beside her chair. "I do love to ride in a parlour car; I wish we were to travel in it for a week."

"I like it, too," agreed Bernice. "Oh, girls, what fun we're going to have! You won't like Uncle Jeff at first, he's awful queer; but there's one thing sure, he'll let us do just as we like. He's very good-natured."

"What's Mrs. Berry like?" asked Dotty. "I suppose we'll obey her?"

"Yes, but she's good-natured, too. I can twist her round my finger. Oh, we'll have a high old time."

" S'pose Mrs. Berry shouldn't be there to meet us when we get in," suggested Dolly. " What then? "

" She will, of course," said Bernice. " But if she shouldn't, if the car broke down or anything like that, we'd take a taxicab right to the house."

This sounded very grown-up and grand to the two D's, who had had little experience with taxicabs, and Dotty exclaimed with glee, " I'd rather do that than go in Mr. Forbes' car! What a lark it would be! Oh, Bernice, can we go somewhere in a taxicab while we're there? "

" I don't know, Dotty,— I s'pose so. But why should we? Uncle Jeff has two cars, and the chauffeur will take us wherever we want to go."

" But I've never been in a taxicab,— without older people, I mean, and I'd love to try it."

" Well, I expect you can," returned Bernice, carelessly. " I dare say you can do pretty much anything you want to."

" But do behave yourself, Dot," cautioned Dolly; " you're so daring and venturesome, I don't know what mischief you'll get into! "

"Oh, we won't get into mischief," laughed Bernice. "There'll be enough fun, without doing anything we oughtn't to."

"Of course, I won't do anything wrong," declared Dotty, indignantly. "But there are so many things to do, it sets me crazy to think of it!"

"I'm going to buy things," announced Bernice. "There aren't any decent shops in Berwick, and I'm going to get lots of things in the city stores."

"We can't do that," said Dolly, decidedly. "We haven't lots of money like you have, Bernie; I'm going to see things. I want to see all the pictures I possibly can. I love to look at pictures."

"I want to go to the theatre," and Dotty looked at Bernice inquiringly. "Will we, do you s'pose?"

"Oh, yes, Mrs. Berry will take us. Perhaps we can go to matinées, alone."

"I don't think we ought to do that," and Dolly looked distinctly disapproving.

"Oh, come now, old priggy-wig," said Dotty, "don't be too awfully 'fraidcat!"

"It will be just as Mrs. Berry says," Bernice informed them. "Father said I must obey her in everything. Uncle Jeff won't pay much attention to what we do, but Mrs. Berry will. I wonder if Alicia will be there when we get there."

But Alicia wasn't. As the girls came up the stairs into the great station, they saw a smiling, motherly-looking lady waiting to welcome them.

"Here you are!" she cried, and it wasn't necessary for Bernice to introduce her friends, except to tell which was which.

"I feel as if I knew you," Mrs. Berry said, and her kindly grey eyes beamed at them both. "Now I must learn to tell you apart. Dolly with golden hair,— Dotty with black. Is that it?"

"Is Alicia here?" asked Bernice, eagerly.

"No; she's coming in at the other station. She won't arrive for an hour or more. Where are your checks? Let George take them."

The footman took the checks and looked after them, while Mrs. Berry piloted the girls to the waiting motor-car.

It was a large and very beautiful limousine, and they all got in, and were soon rolling up Fifth Avenue.

"How splendid it all is!" exclaimed Dolly, looking out at the crowds. "It seems as if we must get all snarled up in the traffic, but we don't."

"Kirke is a very careful driver," said Mrs. Berry, "and he understands just where to go. How you've grown, Bernice. I haven't seen you for two years, you know."

"Yes, I have. We're all getting to be grown-ups, Mrs. Berry. Isn't Alicia?"

"I don't know. I haven't seen her for a long time. But she's at a very fashionable school, so I suppose she is full of notions."

"What are notions?" asked Dolly, smiling up into the speaker's eyes.

"Oh, notions," and Mrs. Berry laughed, "well, it's thinking you know it all yourself, and not being willing to listen to advice. I don't believe you have notions, Dolly."

"No, she hasn't," said Bernice. "But Dotty and I have! However, I promised Dad I'd obey you, Mrs. Berry, in everything you say, so I don't believe you'll have any trouble with us."

"Land, no! I don't expect any. Now, let me

see; I've two big rooms for you all, with two beds in each. I suppose you'll room with your cousin, Bernice, and these other two girls together?"

"Yes, indeed," said Dolly, quickly, for she had no idea of rooming with any one but Dotty.

"That settles itself, then."

"But suppose I don't like Alicia," said Bernice, doubtfully. "Suppose we quarrel."

"All right," and Mrs. Berry nodded her head, "there are other rooms. I don't want you to be uncomfortable in any particular. I thought you'd like it better that way. The two rooms I've fixed for you, are two big ones on the second floor. Mine is on the same floor, in the rear. Your uncle's rooms are upon the third floor."

"I think it sounds fine," declared Bernice, "and I'm sure I'll get on with Alicia, if she does have ' notions.'"

And then they reached the big house on upper Fifth Avenue, and as they entered, Dolly felt a little appalled at the grandeur everywhere about her. Not so Dotty. She loved elegance, and as her feet sank into the deep soft rugs, she laughed out in sheer delight of being in such beautiful surroundings.

-⟨ 36 ⟩-

Mrs. Berry took the girls at once to their rooms, and sent the car for Alicia.

"I'll give the front room to Dotty and Dolly," she said to Bernice; "and you can have the other. It's quite as nice, only it looks out on the side street, not on the Avenue."

"That's right, Mrs. Berry. Dot and Dolly are more company than Alicia and I are. We're really members of the family. I was so surprised at Uncle Jeff's inviting us. Why did he do it, anyway?"

"Why, indeed!" said Mrs. Berry, but her expression was quizzical. "No one can tell why Mr. Forbes does things! He is a law unto himself. Now, girls, your trunks are coming up. And here are two maids to unpack for you and put your things away. You can direct them."

Mrs. Berry bustled away, and two neat-looking maids appeared, one of whom entered Bernice's room and the other attended on Dot and Dolly.

"Which frocks shall I leave out for dinner?" the maid asked, as she shook out and hung up the dresses in the wardrobe.

"The blue voile for me," replied Dolly, "and — er — what is your name?"

"Foster, miss," and she smiled at Dolly's gentle face.

"And the rose-coloured voile for me," directed Dotty. "You'll find, Foster, that our frocks are pretty much alike except as to colour."

"Yes, ma'am. And these patent leather pumps, I daresay?"

"Yes, that's right," and Dotty flung herself into a big easy-chair and sighed in an ecstasy of delight that she really had a ladies' maid to wait on her. Dolly didn't take it so easily. She wanted to look after her own things, as she did at home. But Dotty motioned to her not to do so, lest Foster should think them inexperienced or countrified.

Their simple belongings were soon in place, and the two D's wandered into Bernice's room.

Here everything was helter-skelter. Finery was piled on beds and chairs, and hats were flung on top of one another, while shoes and veils, gloves and hairbrushes were scattered on the floor.

"It's my fault," laughed Bernice, "don't blame Perkins for it! I'm hunting for a bracelet, that has slipped out of my jewel case, somehow. It must be in this lot of stockings!"

It wasn't, but it turned up at last, inside of a hat, and Bernice gave a little squeal of relief.

"That's all right, then!" she cried; "I wouldn't lose that for worlds! It's a bangle father gave me for Christmas, and it has a diamond in the pendant. All right, Perkins, put the things away any place you like. But save hooks and shelves enough for my cousin Alicia. She'll be in this room with me."

Each large room had what seemed to the two little women ample room for clothes. But Bernice had brought so much more than they did, that her things overflowed the space provided.

"I'll wear this to-night, for dinner," she said, pulling out a light green silk from a pile of frocks.

"Oh, Bernie!" exclaimed Dotty; "not that! That's a party dress, isn't it?"

"Not exactly. I've more dressy ones. But it *is* a little fussy for a quiet evening at home, I suppose. Well, what shall I wear?"

"This?" and Dotty picked out a simple challie.

"Oh, gracious, no! That's a morning frock. I guess I'll stick to the green. Don't you think so, Perkins?"

"Yes, miss. It's a lovely gown." The maid was

interested in the girls, her life in the quiet house being usually most uneventful. This sudden invasion of young people was welcomed by all the servants, and there were many in Jefferson Forbes' palatial home. Mrs. Berry had engaged several extra ones to help with the increased work, but the two maids assigned to the girls were trusted and tried retainers.

And then, there was a bustle heard downstairs, a peal of laughter and a perfect flood of chatter in a high, shrill voice, and with a bounding run up the staircase, Alicia burst into the room where the three girls were.

" Hello, Bernice, old girl! " she shouted, and flung her arms around her cousin's neck, giving her resounding smacks on her cheek. " Golly! Molly! Polly! but I'm glad to see you again! Forgotten me, have you? Take a good look! Your long lost Alicia! 'Tis really she! And look who's here! I'll bet a pig these two stammering, blushing young misses are the far-famed Dolly and Dotty, but which is which? "

" Guess! " said Dotty, laughing, as Dolly stood dismayed, and half frightened at this whirlwind of a girl.

" All right, I'll guess. Lemmesee! Dolly Fayre
and Dotty Rose; — you see I know your names.
Why, the fair one is Dolly of course, and that leaves
Dotty to be you!"

" Right!" cried Dotty, and Alicia flew to her and
grabbed her as enthusiastically as she had Bernice.

" Oh, you chickabiddy!" she cried. "I foresee
we shall be chums! I love Towhead, too, but I'm a
little afraid of her. See her steely blue eyes, even
now, fixed on me in utter disapprobation!"

" Not at all," said Dolly, politely, "I think you're
very nice."

The calm demureness of this speech was too much
for Alicia, and she went off in peals of laughter.

" Oh, you're rich!" she cried; "simpully rich!
Won't we have fun! I'm 'most afraid I'll love you
more'n the other one — the black haired witch."
And then Dolly was treated to an embrace that ruf-
fled her hair and collar and came near ruffling her
temper. For Dolly didn't like such sudden familiar-
ity, but her good manners kept her from showing
her annoyance.

" Oh, you don't fool me!" cried Alicia; "I know
you think I'm awful! Too rambunctious and all

-≺ 41 ≻-

that! But I'm used to it! At school they call me That Awful Alicia! How's that?"

"Fine, if you like it — and I believe you do!" laughed Dolly.

"Mind reader! I say, Bernice, where am I to put my togs! You've squatted on every available foot of property in this room! I thought it was to be ours together! But every single bed in the room is covered with your rags. I've two trunks of duds, myself."

"Two trunks! Why did you bring so much?"

"Had to have it. There's lots of things I carry around with me beside clothes. Why, I've brought a whole chafing-dish outfit."

"Goodness, Alicia," exclaimed Bernice, "do you think Uncle Jeff won't give us enough to eat?"

"I take no chances. But it isn't that. It's thusly. Say we're out of an evening, and on returning, are sent straight to beddy-by. How comforting to have the necessary for a little spread of our own! Oh, I've tried it out at school, and I can tell you there's something in it. But, where, ladies and gentlemen, *where* I ask you, can I put it? Bernice has all the places full."

-⟨ 42 ⟩-

" Leave it in your trunk," suggested Dolly, " until you want to use it."

" Angel child!" cried Alicia. " I knew you had some brain concealed among that mop of yellow silk floss! I'll do that same, and be thankful if my voracious cousin leaves me enough room for a few scant and skimpy clodings!"

And then, as Perkins unpacked Alicia's trunks and Foster came in to help, the room really seemed incapable of holding all.

" We'd better get out, Doll," said Dotty, laughing, as Alicia deposited an armful of petticoats and dressing jackets in her lap.

" Oh, don't go! I want you to hold things till I find a place for them. And, say, are your own wardrobes full?"

" No!" cried Dolly. " Just the thing! Put your overflow in our room, we've less than a dozen dresses between us."

" Goodness gracious me! Oh, you're going to buy a lot in the city,— I see!"

" No, we're not," said Dolly, who never sailed under false colours; " we brought all we had, all our best ones, I mean. But we don't have things like you and Bernice."

"You frank little bunch of honesty! Isn't she the darling! All right, neighbours, since you insist, I'll put some seventeen or twenty-four of my Paris confections in your empty cupboards."

Of course, Alicia was exaggerating, but she really did take half a dozen frocks into the two D's room, and hung them in outspread fashion right over their best costumes.

"And, now, since one good turn deserves another," she rattled on, "I'll just toss my extra shoes and slippers into your lowest bureau drawer, and my stockings into the next one. There's plenty of room."

So there was, by crowding the contents already there. But Alicia was so quick of motion, and so gay of speech that they couldn't refuse to let her have her way. And, too, it seemed inevitable, for there wasn't room for Alicia's things and Bernie's in the same room, and the D's shelves and bureau drawers showed much vacancy.

"Now, what do we wear this evening?" Alicia asked, tossing over her dresses. "This, let us say?"

She held up a low-necked evening gown of silk tissue.

"No, you goose," said Bernice, decidedly. "Your respected uncle would think you were crazy! Here, wear this."

Bernice picked out one of the least ornate, a pretty Dresden silk, and then the girls all began to dress for dinner.

CHAPTER IV

A MERRY QUARTETTE

"READY for dinner, girls?" sounded a cheery voice, and Mrs. Berry came bustling in. "Almost, aren't you? Try to remember that Mr. Forbes doesn't like to be kept waiting."

"I'm scared to death," said Bernice, frankly. "I never know what to say to Uncle Jeff, anyway, and being a guest makes it all the harder."

"Pooh! I'm not afraid," exclaimed Alicia. "Leave it to me. I'll engineer the conversation and all you girls need to do is to chip in now and then."

Alicia was a tall, fair girl, larger than any of the others. She was plump and jolly-looking, and had a breezy manner that was attractive because of her smiling good-natured face. She laughed a great deal, and seemed to have no lack of self-confidence and self-assurance. Her dress had many fluttering ribbons of vivid pink, and frills of lace of an inexpensive varity.

She led the way downstairs, calling out, "March

on, march on to victory!" and the others followed.

The four entered the drawing-room, and found there a tall, dignified gentleman, in full evening dress. He had a handsome face, though a trifle stern and forbidding of expression, and his closely trimmed white beard was short and pointed. He had large, dark eyes, which darted from one girl to the other as the quartette appeared.

"H'm," he said, "this is Bernice; how do you do, my dear? How do you do?"

"I'm Alicia," announced that spry damsel, gaily, and she caught him by the hand.

"Yes, and very like your mother, my dear sister. Well, Alicia, if you possess half her fine traits, you'll make a splendid woman. But I doubt if you are very much like her except in appearance. You look to me like a flibbertigibbet,— if you know what that is."

"Yes, and I am one, thank you, Uncle Jeff," and Alicia laughed gaily, not at all abashed at her uncle's remark.

"These are my two friends from Berwick, uncle," said Bernice, introducing them. "Dolly Fayre and Dotty Rose."

"You are welcome, my dears," and the courteous old gentleman bowed to them with great dignity. "I trust you can find amusement and enjoy your visit here. Now, let us dine."

Dolly looked curiously at her host, as he stood back, and bowed the girls out of the room, before he followed them, but Dotty was so interested in the surroundings that she gave no second thought to Mr. Forbes, as she passed him.

The dining-room was a marvel of old time grandeur. Nothing was modern, but the heavy black walnut sideboard and chairs spoke of long usage and old time ways.

Mrs. Berry did not appear at the table, and evidently was not expected, as no place was set for her.

Mr. Forbes sat at the head, and two girls at either side. A grave-faced, important looking butler directed the service, and two footmen assisted. Everything was of the best, and wonderfully cooked and served, but Dolly and Dotty could scarcely eat for the novelty and interest of the scence.

"Come, come, Miss Fayre, eat your terrapin," counselled Mr. Forbes, "it is not so good cold."

"Oh, gracious, Uncle Jeff," exclaimed the vola-

tile Alicia, " don't call those kids Miss! Call 'em
Dotty and Dolly, do."

" Can't remember which is which," declared her
uncle, looking at the two D's. " I can remember the
last names, because the Fayre girl is fair, and the
Rose girl is rosy. I shall call them Rosy and Fairy,
I think."

" All right, Mr. Forbes," and Dolly smiled and
dimpled at the pretty conceit.

" And you two must call me something less
formal," he said. " Suppose you call me Uncle
Forbes, as you are not really my nieces."

This seemed a fine plan and was readily adopted.

" And now," Mr. Forbes went on, " I don't mind
confessing that I've no idea what to do with you
girls. By way of entertainment, I mean."

" Oh, Uncle Jeff," said Bernice, " it's enough entertainment just to be here in New York for a week.
Why, we will have all we can do to see the shops and
the sights — I suppose we can go around sight-
seeing? "

" Bless my soul, yes. Of course you can. Go
where you like. Order the motors whenever you
choose. Mrs. Berry will do all you want her to;

just tell her your plans. All I ask is that I shan't be troubled with you during the day."

"Why, uncle," cried Alicia, "won't we see you at all in the daytime?"

"No. I am a very busy man. I cannot have my work interrupted by a pack of foolish chatterers."

"Whatever did you ask us for?" Alicia's round face wore a look of surprised inquiry.

"Never you mind, miss. I had a very good reason for asking you, but one doesn't always tell his reasons. However, I expect to see you every night at the dinner table, and for an hour or so afterward in the drawing room. The rest of the time you must amuse yourselves. Have you any friends in New York, any of you?"

"I have a few," said Dotty, as the inquiring glance turned in her direction.

"Invite them to the house when you choose," said Mr. Forbes, hospitably, if curtly.

"Oh, no, sir," said Dotty, quickly. "They wouldn't fit in."

Mr. Forbes chuckled. "You have a sense of the fitness of things, Miss Rosy. Why wouldn't they fit in?"

"Why, they're plain people. Not grand and elegant like you."

"Oho! So I'm grand and elegant, am I? And are you grand and elegant, too?"

Dotty considered. "Yes," she said, finally, "I am, while I'm here. I'm very adaptable, and while I'm in New York, I mean to be just as grand and elegant as the house itself."

Mr. Forbes burst into hearty laughter. "Good for you!" he cried. "When you're in Rome do as the Romans do. And you, Fairy of the golden curls. Are you going to be grand, also?"

"I can't," returned Dolly, simply. "I can only be myself, wherever I am. But I shall enjoy all the beautiful things as much as Dotty."

Again Mr. Forbes laughed. "You're a great pair," he said. "I'm glad I discovered you. And now, Bernice and Alicia, haven't you any young friends in town you'd like to invite to see you here? Remember the house is yours."

"Oh, Uncle Jeff," cried Alicia, "you are too good! Do you mean it? Can we do just as we like? Invite parties, and all that?"

"Yes, indeed. Why not? Have the best time

possible, and see to it that those two little friends of yours have a good time, too."

"But won't you go with us anywhere?" asked Bernice; "I thought you'd take us to see places where we can't go alone."

"Bless my soul! Take a lot of chattering magpies sightseeing! No, not if I know it! Mrs. Berry will take you; and on a pinch, I might let my secretary accompany you, say to see the downtown big buildings or the bright lights at night."

"Oh, do you have a secretary?" asked Alicia. "What's he like?"

"Fenn? Oh, he's a good sort. Very dependable and really accommodating. He'll be of great help to you, I'm sure."

"What is your business, Mr. Forbes?" asked Dolly, who was much interested in this strange type of man. She had never seen any one like him, and he seemed to her a sort of fairy godfather, who waved his wand and gave them all sorts of wonderful gifts.

"I haven't any business, my dear. My occupation and amusement is collecting specimens for my collection. I am an entomologist and ornithologist, if you know what those big words mean."

"Yes, sir, I do." And Dolly smiled back at him. "Mayn't we see your collection?"

"I'm not sure about that. I don't show it to everybody. It is up on the fourth floor of this house, and no one is allowed up there unless accompanied by myself or Mr. Fenn. By the way, remember that, all of you. On no account go up to the fourth floor. Not that you'd be likely to, for you have no call above the second floor, where your rooms are. But this is a special command. The house is yours, as I said, but that means only this first floor and the one above it."

"Goodness me, Uncle Jeff!" said Alicia, "you needn't lay down the law so hard! We're not absolute babes, to be so strictly cautioned and forbidden! If you desire us not to go up the second flight of stairs, of course we won't."

"That's right, my dear, don't. But I do lay it down as a law, and it is the only law I shall impose on you. Except for that you can follow out your own sweet wills."

" But," said Dotty, her dark eyes brilliant with the excitement of the occasion, " I'm not always sure as to what is proper. I want to do just what is right. Is it correct for us to go about alone, in your big motor, with your chauffeur? Can we go to the art galleries and the shops alone? "

" Bless my soul! I don't know." The big man looked absolutely helpless. " Surely you must know such things yourselves. What do your mothers let you do at home? Oh, well, if you're uncertain, ask Mrs. Berry, she'll know. She's an all-round capable person, and she'll know all the unwritten laws about chaperonage and such things. Do as she bids you."

This was satisfactory, and Dotty began at once to make plans for the next day.

" Let's go to the Metropolitan Museum first," she said.

" All right," chimed in Alicia, " we'll go there in the morning, then. But to-morrow is Wednesday, and I want to go to a matinée in the afternoon. Can't we, Uncle Jeff? "

" Of course you can. Tell Fenn, he'll see about tickets for you. Just tell Mrs. Berry to see Fenn about it."

" Oh," sighed the outspoken Dotty, " it is just like Fairyland! Tell Fenn! Just as if Fenn were a magician!"

" He is," said Mr. Forbes, smiling at her enthusiasm. " I couldn't keep house without Fenn. He's my right hand man for everything. You girls mustn't claim too much of his time and attention, for I keep him on the jump most of the time myself."

" Does your collection keep you so busy?" asked Dolly, whose secret longing was to see that same collection, which greatly interested her.

"Yes, indeed. There's always work to be done in connection with it. I've a lot of new specimens just arrived to-day, awaiting classification and tabulation."

After dinner they all returned to the drawing-room. Mr. Forbes seemed desirous of keeping up a general conversation, but it was hard to find a subject to interest him. He would talk a few moments, and then lapse into absent-mindedness and almost forget the girls' presence.

At times, he would get up from his chair, and stalk up and down the room, perhaps suddenly pausing in front of one of them, and asking a direct question.

"How old are you?" he asked abruptly of Alicia.

"Sixteen," she replied. "I was sixteen last October."

"You look like your mother at that age. She was my only sister. She has now been dead —"

"Ten years," prompted Alicia. "I was a little child when she died."

"And who looks after you now? Your father's sister, isn't it?"

"Yes, Uncle Jeff. My Aunt Nellie. But I'm at school, you know. I shall be there the next four years, I suppose."

"Yes, yes, to be sure. Yes, yes, of course. And you, Bernice? You have no mother, either. But who looks after you?"

"I look after myself, Uncle. Father thinks there's no necessity for me to have a chaperon in our little home town."

"Not a chaperon, child, but you ought to have some one to guide and teach you."

"Dad doesn't think so. He says an American girl can take care of herself."

"Maybe so, maybe so. It might be a good thing for you to go to school with Alicia."

"It might be. But I like our High School at home, and we learn a lot there."

"But not the same kind of learning. Do they teach you manners and general society instruction?"

"No," said Bernice, smiling at thought of such things in connection with the Berwick school. "But my father thinks those things come naturally to girls of good families."

"Maybe so, maybe so." And then Mr. Forbes again walked up and down the long room, seemingly lost in his own thoughts.

Dolly and Dotty felt a little uncomfortable. They wanted to make themselves agreeable and entertaining, but their host seemed interested exclusively in his young relatives, and they hesitated lest they intrude.

As it neared ten o'clock, Mr. Forbes paused in his pacing of the room, bowed to each of the four in turn, and then saying, courteously, "I bid you good-night," he vanished into the hall.

Immediately Mrs. Berry entered. It seemed a relief to see her kind, smiling face after the uncertain phases of their eccentric host.

"Now you young people must go to bed," the housekeeper said; "you're tired,— or ought to be. Come along."

Not at all unwillingly they followed her upstairs, and she looked after their comfort in most solicitous fashion.

After she had shown them how to ring the various bells to call the maids or to call her, in emergency, and had drawn their attention to the ice water in thermos bottles, and told them how to adjust the ventilators, she bade them good-night and went away.

The rooms had a communicating door, and this Alicia promptly threw open and came through into the two D's room.

"Oh, isn't it all the greatest fun! And did you *ever* see anything so crazy as Uncle Jeff? What he wants us here for, *I* don't know! But it's something, — and something especial. He never asked us here to amuse him! Of that I'm certain."

"Not much he didn't!" and Bernice followed Alicia, and perched on the edge of Dolly's bed. "Isn't he queer? I didn't know he was so funny as he is. Did you, Alicia?"

" No; I haven't seen him since I was a tiny mite. But he's all right. He knows what he's about and I don't wonder he doesn't want us bothering around if he's busy."

" I'd love to see his collection," said Dolly. " I'm awfully interested in such things."

" Oh, well, you'll probably have a chance to see it while we're here," and Alicia began taking down her hair. " Now, girls, let's get to bed, for I'm jolly well tired out. But I foresee these poky evenings right along, don't you? We'll have to cram a lot of fun into our days, if the evenings are to be spent watching an elderly gentleman stalking around thus." And then Alicia gave a very good imitation of the way Mr. Forbes walked around. She didn't ridicule him; she merely burlesqued his manner as he paused to speak to them in his funny, abrupt way.

" What are you, my dear? " she said, looking at Dolly. " Are you a specimen I can use in my collection? No? Are you a fashionable butterfly? I say, Bernice," she suddenly broke off, " why was he so curious about the way we live at home, and who brings us up? "

" I don't know; and anyway, he knew how long our

mothers have been dead and who takes care of us. Why did he ask those things over and over? "

" I think he's a bit absent-minded. Half the time he was thinking of matters far removed from this charming quartette of bewitching beauties. Well, it's up to us to make our own good time. I move we corral the big limousine for to-morrow morning and go in search of adventure."

" To the Metropolitan? " suggested Dolly.

" Yes, if you like, though I'd rather go to the shops," and Alicia gathered up her hairpins to depart. Her long light hair hung round her shoulders, and she pushed it back as she affectionately kissed Dolly and Dotty good-night. " You are sure two darlings! " she said emphatically.

CHAPTER V

FOUR smiling, eager girls trooped down to breakfast the next morning, and found Mrs. Berry awaiting them. She presided at the table, and they learned that she would always do so at breakfast and luncheon, though she did not dine with them.

"Uncle Jeff says we may go to a matinée to-day," said Alicia, delightedly. "Will you see about the tickets, Mrs. Berry? Uncle said Mr. Fenn would get them if you asked him to."

"Yes, my dear. And what are your plans for the morning? Do you want the car?"

"Yes, indeed," said Bernice. "We're going to the Museum and I don't know where else."

"To the Library, if we have time," suggested Dolly. "I want to see all the places of interest."

"Places of interest never interest me," declared Alicia. "I think they're poky."

"All right," returned Dolly, good-naturedly, "I'll go wherever you like."

-◖ 61 ◗-

"Now, don't be so ready to give in, Doll," cautioned Bernice. "You have as much right to your way as Alicia has to hers."

"No, I haven't," and Dolly smiled brightly; "this is the house of Alicia's uncle, and not mine."

"Well, he's my uncle, too, and what I say goes, as much as Alicia's commands."

"There, there, girls, don't quarrel," said Mrs. Berry, in her amiable way. "Surely you can all be suited. There are two cars, you know, and if you each want to go in a different direction, I'll call taxicabs for you."

Dolly and Dotty stared at this new lavishness, and Dotty said, quickly, "Oh, no, don't do that! We all want to be together, wherever we go. And I think, as Dolly does, that Bernice and Alicia must choose, for they belong here and we're guests."

"You're two mighty well-behaved little guests," and Mrs. Berry beamed at them. "Well, settle it among yourselves. Now, what matinée do you want to go to? I'll order tickets for you."

"Will you go with us, Mrs. Berry?" asked Dolly.

"No, child. I hope you'll let me off. You girls are old enough to go alone in the daytime, and Kirke will take you and come to fetch you home. Now, what play?"

"I want to see 'The Lass and the Lascar'; that's a jolly thing, I hear," said Alicia, as no one else suggested anything.

"Musical?" asked Bernice.

"Yes," said Mrs. Berry, "it's a comic opera, and a very good one. I've seen it, and I'm sure you girls will enjoy it. I'll order seats for that. Be sure to be home for luncheon promptly at one, so you can get ready for the theatre."

"I can't believe it all," whispered Dotty, pinching Dolly's arm, as they ran upstairs to prepare for their morning's trip. "Think of our going to all these places in one day!"

"And six days more to come!" added Dolly. "Oh, it is too gorgeous!"

Arrayed in warm coats and furs, the laughing quartette got into the big car, and George, the polite footman, adjusted the robes, and asked their destination.

"To the Metropolitan Museum, first," said Alicia, unselfishly.

"Oh," cried Dolly, with sparkling eyes, "are we

really going there first! How good of you, Alicia!"

And from the moment they entered the vestibule of the great museum, Dolly was enthralled with what she saw. Like one in a trance, she walked from room to room, drinking in the beauty or strangeness of the exhibits. She ignored the catalogues, merely gazing at the pictures or curios with an absorbed attention that made her oblivious to all else.

"Watch her," said Alicia, nudging Dotty. "She doesn't even know where she is! Just now, she's back in Assyria with the people that wore that old jewellery!"

Sure enough Dolly was staring into a case of antique bracelets and earrings of gold and jewels. She moved along the length of the case, noting each piece, and fairly sighing with admiration and wonder.

"My gracious! isn't she the antiquarian!" exclaimed Alicia. "Look here, old Professor Wiseacre, what dynasty does this junk belong to?"

Dolly looked up with a vacant stare.

"Come back to earth!" cried Alicia, shaking with laughter. "Come back to the twentieth century! We mourn our loss!"

" Yes, come back, Dollums," said Dotty. " There are other rooms full of stuff awaiting your approval."

Dolly laughed. " Oh, you girls don't appreciate what you're seeing. Just think! Women wore these very things! Real, live women!"

" Well, they're not alive now," said Bernice, " and we are. So give us the pleasure of your company. Say, Dolly, some day you come up here all alone by yourself, and prowl around —"

" Oh, I'd love to! I'll do just that. And then I won't feel that I'm delaying you girls. Where do you want to go now?"

" Anywhere out of this old museum," said Alicia, a little pettishly. " You've had your way, Dotty, now it's only fair I should have mine. We've about an hour left; let's go to the shops."

" Yes, indeed," and Dolly spoke emphatically. " I didn't realise that I was being a selfish old piggy-wig!"

" And you're not," defended Bernice. 'We all wanted to come here, but, well, you see, Dolly, you do dawdle."

" But it's such a wonder-place!" and Dolly gazed

longingly backward as they left the antiquities. "And there are rooms we haven't even looked into yet."

"Dozens of 'em," assented Alicia. "But not this morning, my chickabiddy! I must flee to the busy marts and see what's doing in the way of tempting bargains."

"All right," and Dolly put her arm through Alicia's. "What are you going to buy?"

"Dunno, till I see something that strikes my fancy. But in the paper this morning, I noticed a special sale of 'Pastime Toggery' at Follansbee's. Let's go there."

"Never heard of the place," said Dolly. "But let's go."

"Never heard of Follansbee's! Why, it's the smartest shop in New York for sport clothes."

"Is it? We never get sport clothes. Unless you mean middies and sweaters. My mother buys those at the department stores."

"Oh, you can't get exclusive models there!" and Alicia's face wore a reproving expression.

"No," said outspoken Dolly, "but we don't **wear**

-⟡ 66 ⟡-

exclusive models. We're rather inclusive, I expect."

"You're a duck!" cried Alicia, who, though ultra-fashionable herself, liked the honesty and frankness of the two D's.

They reached the shop in question, and the four girls went in.

The Berwick girls were a little awed at the atmosphere of the place, but Alicia was entirely mistress of the situation.

She had many costumes and accessories shown to her, and soon became as deeply absorbed in their contemplation as Dolly had been in the Museum exhibits.

"Why, for goodness' sake!" cried Bernice, at last. "Are you going to buy out the whole shop, Alicia?"

"Why, I'm not going to buy any," returned Alicia, looking surprised; "I'm just shopping, you know."

"Oh, is that it? Well, let me tell you it isn't any particular fun for us to look on while you 'shop'! And, anyway, it's time to be going home, or we'll be late for the luncheon and for the matinée."

"All right, I'll go now. But wait, I want to buy some little thing for you girls,— sort of a souvenir, you know."

"Good for you!" said Bernice, but Dolly demurred.

"I don't think you ought to, Alicia," she said. "I don't believe my mother would like me to take it."

"Nonsense, Towhead! I'm just going to get trifles. Nobody could object to my giving you a tiny token of my regard and esteem. Let me see,— how about silk sweaters? They're always handy to have in the house."

Unheeding the girls' protestations, Alicia selected four lovely colours, and asked the saleswoman to get the right sizes.

Dolly's was robin's egg blue; Dotty's salmon pink; Bernice's, a deep orange, and Alicia's own was white, as she declared she already had every colour of the rainbow.

Then she selected an old rose one for Mrs. Berry, getting permission to exchange it if it should be a misfit.

Alicia ordered the sweaters sent to her uncle's house, and the bill sent to her father. This arrange-

ment seemed perfectly satisfactory to the shop people, and the girls set off for home.

"I feel uncomfortable about that sweater," announced Dolly, as they were on their way.

"That doesn't matter," laughed Alicia, "so long
as you don't feel uncomfortable in it! Remove that
anxious scowl, my little Towhead; I love to give
things to my friends, and you must learn to accept
trifles gracefully."

"But it isn't a trifle, Alicia. I know mother
won't like it."

"Won't like that blue sweater! Why, it's a
beauty!"

"I don't mean that. I mean she won't like for me
to take it,— to accept it from you."

"All right; tell her you bought it yourself."

"Tell a story about it! No, thank you." Dolly's
blue eyes fairly flashed at the thought.

"Well, my stars! Dolly, don't make such a fuss
about it! Throw it away, or give it to the scullery
maid! You don't have to keep it!"

Clearly, Alicia was annoyed. Dolly was far from
ungrateful, and she didn't know quite what to do.

"Of course, she'll keep it," Dotty broke in, anxious to straighten matters out. "She adores it, Alicia; but we girls aren't accustomed to making each other gifts,— at least, not expensive ones."

"Well, you needn't make a habit of it. One sweater doesn't make a summer! I hope Mrs. Berry won't be so squeamish! If I thought she would, I'd throw hers in the ash barrel before I'd give it to her!"

"I s'pose I was horrid about it, Alicia," said Dolly, contritely; "I do love it, really, you know I do; but, as Dotty says, we never give such gifts. Why, I can't give you anything to make up for it —"

"And I don't want you to! You little goose! But like as not, you can sometime do something for me worth more than a dozen sweaters."

"I hope so, I'm sure. Will you tell me if I can?"

"Yes, baby-face! I declare, Dolly, it's hard to realise you're fifteen years old! You act about twelve,— and look ten!"

"Oh, not so bad as that!" and Dolly laughed gaily. "I s'pose I do seem younger than I am, because I've always lived in a small town. We don't do things like city girls."

"'Deed we don't!" exclaimed Dotty. "I used to

live in the city, and when I went to Berwick it was like a different world. But I've come to like it now."

"I like it," said Bernice, decidedly. "I think we have a lot more fun in Berwick than we could in New York. To live, I mean. Of course, this visit here is lovely, but it's the novelty and the strange sights that make it so. I wouldn't want to live in New York."

"Neither would I," and Dolly shook her head very positively.

"I would," said Alicia. "I'd just love to live here, in a house like Uncle Jeff's, and have all these cars and servants and everything fine."

"No, thank you," Dolly rejoined. "It's beautiful for a week, but it makes my head go round to think of living like this always."

"Your head is not very securely fastened on, anyway," and Alicia grinned at her. "You'll lose it some day!"

"Maybe so," smiled Dolly, affably, and then they suddenly found they were back home.

"Good time, girlies?" called out Mrs. Berry, as they entered. "Lunch is all ready; sit down and eat it, and get dressed for the matinée afterward. Mr. Fenn got fine seats for you,— near the front. You'll like the play, I know."

And like the play they did. It was a light opera, of the prettiest type, full of lovely scenery, gay costumes and bright, catchy music. "The Lass and the Lascar" was its name, and the lass in question was a charming little girl who seemed no older than the quartette themselves. The Lascar was a tall, handsome man, whose swarthy East Indian effects were picturesque and attractive. He had a magnificent baritone voice, and the girls sat breathless when he sang his splendid numbers. All four were fond of music and even more than the gay splendour of the show they enjoyed the voices and orchestra.

"Isn't he wonderful!" exclaimed Alicia, as the curtain fell on the first act. "Oh, girls, isn't he *superb!* I'm *madly* in love with him!"

"He has a beautiful voice," agreed Dolly, "but I couldn't be in love with him! He's too,— too ferocious!"

"But that's his charm," declared Alicia, rolling her eyes in ecstasy. "Oh, he is ideal! He's fascinating!"

The curtain rose again, and the Lascar proved even more fascinating. He was a daredevil type, as Lascars have the reputation of being, but he was gentle and affectionate toward the Lass, who, for some inexplicable reason, scorned his advances.

" What a *fool* she is! *What* a fool! " Alicia whispered, as the coquettish heroine laughed at the impassioned love songs of her suitor. " I should fall into his arms at once! "

" Then there wouldn't be any more opera," laughed Bernice. " That fall into his arms is always the last episode on the stage."

" That's so," agreed Alicia, " but how can she flout him so? Oh, girls, isn't he the grandest man? I never saw such a handsome chap! What a lovely name he has, too: Bayne Coriell! A beautiful name."

" Good gracious, Alicia! don't rave over him like that! Somebody will hear you! "

" I don't care. I never saw any one so wonderful! I'm going to get his picture when we go out. I suppose it's for sale in the lobby. They usually are."

" Are they? " asked Dolly. " Then I want to get

one of the Lass. Marie Desmond, her name is. Can I, do you think? "

" Yes, of course, Dollykins. You get that and I'll get my hero, my idol, Bayne Coriell! "

As it chanced the photographs were not on sale at the theatre, but an usher told Alicia where they could be bought, and she directed Kirke to stop there on the way home.

She bought several different portraits of the man who had so infatuated her and Dolly bought two photographs of Miss Desmond. The other girls said they didn't care for any pictures, and laughed at the enthusiasm of Alicia and Dolly.

" I want this," Dolly defended herself, " because sometime I'm going to be an opera singer. I did mean to sing in Grand Opera, and maybe I will, but if I can't do that, I'll sing in light opera, and I like to have this picture to remind me how sweet Miss Desmond looks in this play."

" Pooh," said Alicia, " that's all very well. But I want these pictures of Bayne Coriell because he's such a glorious man! Why, he's as handsome as Apollo. And, girls, I don't believe he's hardly any older than we are."

"Oh, he must be," returned Dotty. "Why, he's twenty-two or more, I'm sure."

"Maybe he is twenty, but not more than that. Oh, how I wish I could meet him! Think of the joy of talking to a man like that!"

"Well, it's not likely you'll ever meet Bayne Coriell," said Bernice, laughing at the idea; "so you needn't hope for that!"

CHAPTER VI

A MATINEE IDOL

"OH, Uncle Jeff," Alicia cried, as they gathered round the dinner-table that same night, "we went to the splendidest play! It was a light opera, 'The Lass and the Lascar.' Have you seen it?"

"No, my dear, I rarely go to the theatre; never to foolish pieces like that! But it's all right for you young people. So you enjoyed it, did you? How did you like —"

But Alicia's babble interrupted him. "Oh, Uncle, it was simply out of sight! And the hero! Ah-h-h!"

Alicia leaned back in her chair and closed her eyes as if the memory of the hero was overwhelming.

"Took your fancy, did he?" asked her uncle, with a twinkle in his eye. "Good-looking chap?"

"Good-looking faintly expresses it!" and Alicia

returned to consciousness. "He was like a Greek god! And his *charm!* Oh, Uncle Jeff, he is just indescribable! I wish you could *see* him."

"Must be a paragon! What did the rest of you girls think! Were you hit so hard?"

Dotty laughed. "He was splendid, Uncle Forbes," she said, "but we didn't fall so head over heels in love with him as Alicia did. He has a stunning voice and he's a fine actor."

"Oh, more than that!" raved Alicia. "He's a *darling!* a man of a *thousand!*"

"A young man?" asked Mr. Forbes.

"Yes," replied Bernice. "Alicia thinks he isn't twenty, but he can't be much more. He looked a mere boy."

"Wasn't that because he was made up as a young character in the play?"

"Partly," admitted Alicia. "But he's a very young man, anyway. Oh, Uncle Jeff, I'm just *crazy* over him! I think I shall go to see that play every chance I can possibly get. Could we go to an evening performance?"

"Speak for yourself, John!" cried Bernice. "I don't want to see that play again! I enjoyed it heaps, and I think Mr. Coriell was fine, but next time we go I'd rather see something else."

" So would I," said the two D's together.

" How can you say so!" and Alicia looked at the others in scorn. " You'll never find any actor who can hold a candle to Coriell! I have his picture, Uncle," and, excusing herself, she left the table to get them.

" H'm, yes, a good-looking man," agreed Mr. Forbes, as he scrutinised the photographs. " But, Alicia, you mustn't fall in love with every operatic tenor you see. I believe this Coriell is a ' matinée idol,' but don't allow him to engage your young affections."

" Too late with your advice, Uncle Jeff!" and Alicia gazed raptly at the pictures. " I *adore* him! and the fact that my adoration is hopeless makes it all the more interesting. Oh, isn't he a *wonder!* "

Gaily she set the pictures up in front of her, propping them on glasses or salt cellars, and continued to make mock worship at his shrine.

" Don't be silly, Alicia," commented her uncle, but she only shook her head at him, and gave a mournful sigh.

The girls spent the evening much the same as they had done the night before. They all sat in the stately drawing-room, and endeavoured to make conversation. But Uncle Jeff was hard to talk to, for he rarely stuck to one subject for more than five minutes at a time, and abruptly interrupted the girls when they were trying their best to be entertaining.

Alicia continued to chatter about her new-found enthusiasm, until her uncle commanded her to desist.

"May I beg of you, Alicia," he said, sternly, "to cease raving over that man? He's doubtless old enough to be your father, and would be bored to death could he hear your nonsense about him!"

Alicia looked put out, but a glance at her uncle's face proved his seriousness, and she said no more about the actor.

The evening wore away, but it seemed to the girls as if it never would be ten o'clock. And it was greatly to their relief, when, at about half-past nine, Mr. Forbes bade them good-night and went off upstairs.

"It is all the queerest performance," said Bernice. "What in the world does Uncle Jeff want of us,— I can't make out. The outlook seems to be that we

can have all the fun we want daytimes, and pay for it
by these ghastly evening sessions."

"There's something back of it all," said Alicia,
astutely. "This revered uncle of ours, Bernie, has
something up his sleeve."

"I think so, too," said Dotty. "He scrutinises
us all so closely, when he thinks we're not looking.
But I, for one, am quite willing to put up with these
evenings for the sake of the fun we have in the daytime."

"I should say so!" agreed Dolly. "We never
can thank you enough, Bern, for bringing us."

"And I'm glad to have you here," said Mrs.
Berry, entering the room. "You're like a ray of sunshine in this dull house,— like four rays of sunshine."

"But *why* are we here?" insisted Alicia. "You
must know why, Mrs. Berry. Do tell us."

"You're here, my dears, because Mr. Forbes invited you. There is no other reason,— no other explanation. And now, tell me, did you like the
play?"

"Did we *like* it!" exclaimed the volatile Alicia,
"we're just crazy over it. Why, the chief actor —"

"Now, 'Licia," protested Dolly, "if you're going to begin raving over that man again!"

"Well, I am!" declared Alicia. "I just can't help it!"

Nor did she seem able to curb her enthusiasm, for after the girls went to their rooms, she kept on extolling Mr. Coriell until the others were tired of the subject.

And even when the D's were nearly ready for bed, and, in kimonos, were brushing their hair, Alicia burst into their room, exclaiming, " I've the grandest plan! I'm going to invite Mr. Coriell to come here and call on me!"

"Alicia Steele!" Dotty cried, "you're not going to do any such thing!"

"Yes, I am. Uncle Jeff said we could invite anybody we wanted to,— that's permission enough for me."

"But he didn't mean some one you don't know at all,— and an actor at that!"

"I don't care. He didn't make any exceptions, and I'm going to do it. I'm going to write the note now."

She went back to her own room, and sat down at the pretty little escritoire that was there.

"How shall I address him?" she asked, but more of herself than the others.

"Not at all!" said Dolly, and she took the pen from Alicia's fingers. "You must be crazy to think of such a thing!"

"Don't do it, Alicia," begged Dotty; "tell her not to, Bernice."

"I don't care what she does," and Bernice laughed. "It's none of my affair. I think it would be rather good fun, only I know he wouldn't come."

"I think he would," said Alicia. "Anyway, I'm going to tell him how I adored his acting and his singing, and I guess he'll be glad to come to call at Jefferson Forbes' house! I think I'll ask him to afternoon tea. Why, it isn't such a terrible thing, as you seem to think, Dolly. Anybody has a right to write to an actor,— they expect it. He probably gets hundreds of notes every day."

"Then he won't notice yours. He can't possibly accept a hundred invitations."

"Oh, they don't all invite him. Any way, I'm going to write."

A MATINEE IDOL

Alicia found another pen, and soon produced this effusion:

"*My dear Mr. Coriell.*

"I'm just simply crazy over your performance in 'The Lass and the Lascar' and I feel that I *must* meet you. I shall *die* if I don't! Please, oh, *please* give me an opportunity. Will you come to see me at my uncle's house, Mr. Jefferson Forbes? Can you come to-morrow or Friday? I can't *exist* if you say No! So grant the plea of

"Your devoted admirer,
"ALICIA STEELE."

"It's perfectly horrid!" and Dolly's fair face grew flushed with anger. "You ought to be ashamed of yourself, Alicia."

"Now, look here, Dolly Fayre," and Alicia's eyes flashed, "I won't be dictated to by a little country ignoramus! I've had experience in the ways of the world, and you haven't. Now suppose you let me alone. It's none of your business, as you very well know."

"Dolly was only advising you for your own good!" Dotty flashed out, indignant at the rebuff to her chum; "but, truly, Doll, it isn't up to you to tell Alicia what to do. This is her uncle's house, not yours, and you're in no way responsible for her doings."

"I know it," and Dolly looked serious, "but I know, too, Alicia will be sorry and ashamed if she sends that silly letter!"

"Let her be, then," counselled Bernice. "If Uncle Jeff doesn't like it, that's Alicia's affair, not ours. Leave her alone, Dolly."

But Dolly made one more effort.

"Listen, Alicia," she said, pleadingly; "at least, ask Mrs. Berry's advice. She's awfully indulgent, you know, and if she says all right,— then go ahead."

Alicia looked at Dolly. To tell the truth, she had misgivings herself about the plan, but she was too proud to be advised.

"I'll tell you what," she decided, at last; "you said, only to-day, Dolly, that you'd be glad to do something for me. Now, prove that you meant it. You go and ask Mrs. Berry if we can do this. She's awfully fond of you, and she'd say yes to you quicker'n she would to me. So, if you're so anxious for her consent, go and ask her. She's in her room, — I just heard her go in."

"But, Alicia," and Dolly looked dismayed, "*I* don't want to do this thing! Why should I ask Mrs. Berry for what *you* want?"

"Because you said you'd be glad to do me a favour. I knew you didn't mean it! I knew you'd fizzle out when the time came!"

"She hasn't fizzled out!" exclaimed Dotty. "Doll never breaks a promise. But, say, Alicia, I'll go and ask Mrs. Berry. How's that?"

"No, Dolly's got to go, if any one does. She said she'd love to do me a favour, now let her do it."

It was evidently a test case with Alicia, and one glance at her determined face convinced Dolly, that she would never be forgiven if she failed to do this thing.

"All right," she said, slowly, "I'll go and ask Mrs. Berry. But I shall tell her it's for you, Alicia. I shan't let her think I want to ask that man here!"

"Hold on, Dolly. Don't you think it would be nice if he should come, with Mrs. Berry's permission?"

"Yes, I think that would be lots of fun; but she won't give permission, Alicia. I know that as well as I know my own name!"

"Of course, she won't, if you go about it that way! I depend on you to coax her or get around her some way to *make* her say yes. See? Don't think that you can go in there and say 'May we?' and have her say 'No,' and let that end it! I tell you you've got to get her consent. You've got to do this for me, because you said you'd do whatever I asked you."

"Oh, Alicia!" and Dotty shook her head vigorously, "Doll never said *that!*"

"Well, she meant that. And what's the use of her doing anything I can do for myself? But you all know she's Mrs. Berry's pet of the four of us —"

"No, I'm not," and Dolly looked deeply troubled.

"Yes, you are, and it's just because you're so mild and meek. Now, will you go and ask her? You'll have to be quick or she'll have gone to bed."

"Yes, I'll go," and Dolly showed sudden determination.

"And will you promise to do all you can to make her say yes —"

"I'll do that, Alicia, but I can't promise to make her say yes."

"You can if you coax her. And don't let her

think it's all for my benefit. Because it isn't. You girls will have just as much fun as I will, if he comes."

Dolly twisted up her golden curls in a loose knot, and still in her trailing dressing-gown, she went down the hall to Mrs. Berry's room and tapped gently at the door.

It was opened at once, and Dolly was glad to see Mrs. Berry had not yet begun her preparations for the night, so she was not disturbing her.

"What is it, dearie?" asked the kind-hearted lady; "come in. Sit down."

Dolly sat down in a little rocker, and was suddenly seized with a fit of shyness. The request she had come to make seemed so impossible, that she couldn't put it into words. Mrs. Berry saw her embarrassment, and kindly strove to put her at ease.

"How do you like my room?" she said, cordially; "you've never been in here before."

"It's lovely," said Dolly, looking about at the pretty furnishings; "it's in a sort of back extension, isn't it?"

"Yes, this a narrower part of the house, and gives me an outlook on our tiny yard as well as on the side street. It's a very satisfactory room, except for my neighbour," and she laughed.

"Who is the unsatisfactory neighbour?" asked Dolly, smiling in response.

"Not the people next door, they're quiet enough; but they have a parrot, and he's in the room just across from this, and he chatters so often that it is sometimes very annoying. Look over, you can see him now."

Sure enough, as Dolly looked from the window, she saw a big Polly in a cage at the opposite casement. Only thin lace curtains were between, and Dolly could clearly see the beautiful bird.

"It's a lovely parrot," she said, "but I suppose his chatter is just as bothersome as if he were a homelier bird. Well, Mrs. Berry," and she turned from the window, "I've come to ask you something."

"And something that you hesitate to ask,— I can see that. But don't be afraid, dear. Tell me what it is, and if I have to refuse you, at least I won't do it harshly."

"I know you won't!" and Dolly felt ashamed of her fears. "Well, it's just this. Alicia,— that is, we're all of us just crazy over the hero in the play we saw this afternoon, and we — that is, we think it would be nice if we could — if we could ask him to — to call here, on us."

The dreaded speech was made, and though Mrs. Berry looked surprised, she didn't exclaim in horror at the idea.

" Whose plan is this? " she asked, quietly.

" Why,— well,— we all want it."

" Yes, but who first thought of it? "

" Alicia spoke of it, and — the others agreed,— we all agreed,— that it would be lots of fun,— if you approved of it."

Now Mrs. Berry could see a hole through a millstone, and she knew as well as if she had been told, that the others had planned this thing,— probably Alicia or Bernice,— and had made Dolly their spokesman, because of her good-natured acquiescence.

" What do *you* think of the idea? " she said smiling.

" At first it seemed to me a very forward thing to do," Dolly replied, looking very sober; " but if you think it's all right, I'd like to meet Mr. Coriell. You see, I'm going to be an opera singer myself, some day, and there are a few questions I'd like to ask him."

Mrs. Berry gasped. "You do beat the dickens!" she exclaimed. "So you're going on the stage, are you?"

"Yes, I think so."

"Then of course you ought to meet an actor. Tell Alicia to go ahead and ask this man. Tell her to invite him to tea on Friday. I'll arrange a pretty tea-party for you."

"Oh, I'll tell her! She'll be *so* glad!" and Dolly departed, quite unconscious that she had unwittingly betrayed Alicia's principal part in the scheme.

CHAPTER VII

GREAT PREPARATIONS

DEMURELY Dolly went back to her room. The other girls were breathlessly awaiting her return, and pounced on her for the news.

"At least you got back alive!" cried Dotty as she grabbed Dolly by the arms and danced her up and down the room.

"But what did she say?" demanded Alicia, in fiery impatience.

"Don't you wish you knew!" and Dolly fell into a teasing mood, and when Dolly Fayre felt like teasing, she was adept at it!

"Tell us! Tell us!" cried Bernice. "Oh, Dolly, tell us!"

"Tell you what?" asked Dolly, with an innocent stare.

"Tell us what Mrs. Berry said."

"Oh, she asked me how I liked her room, and she showed me the parrot next door. It's a beautiful bird—"

"Never mind a bird! What did she say about Mr. Coriell?"

"Why, we talked about the parrot first. You see, his cage hangs in a window right across from hers, not ten feet away —"

"Nonsense!" cried Alicia, "who cares about the parrot! Tell us about my hero!"

"She says he has a dreadful voice, and squawks like fury —"

"Oh, he *hasn't!* He's a wonderful singer!"

"I mean the parrot," said Dolly, mischievously enjoying Alicia's disgusted look. "And she says we can ask him to tea."

"Who? the parrot?" This from Dotty.

"No, you silly! Mr. Coriell. But, of course, if you'd rather have the parrot —"

"Oh, Dolly, do be sensible!" and Bernice looked exasperated; "are you going to tell us all about it or not?"

"Not if you're so rude to me! Certainly not! You are dismissed, you two. Dot and I are going to bed."

"Not much you're not!" declared Alicia. "Not till you tell us what Mrs. Berry said."

"Then you must ask me with due politeness and proper courtesy. I can't report to a lot of cackling geese! You're worse than parrots!"

"Please, dear, sweet Dollyrinda, what *did* the lady say?" begged Dotty, in wheedling tones.

"Ah, yes, tell us," and Alicia took the cue. "Angel child! Beautiful blonde Towhead! what,— oh, vouchsafe to deign to tell us, *what* did she say?"

"Whoop it up, Dollums," said Bernice, laughing, "out with it, you little rascal. Did she hold up her hands in horror?"

"She did *not*," said Dolly, with dignity. "She said, that if Alicia chose, she might invite the gentleman to tea on Friday, and that she would see to it that there was a nice tea-party prepared for his benefit. There, *who's* a good ambassador?"

"You are! you blessed angel!" cried Alicia, warmly; "you're a wonder! a marvel! a peach! a pippin! Oh, you're just all there is of it! Did she *really* say that?"

"Oh, you want to know what she *really* said," and Dolly's head went on one side, as she began to tease again.

"Of course, that's what she really said," interposed Dotty, who didn't want any more high words. "'Licia, be satisfied with that, and scoot to bed."

"Nothing of the sort. We're going to make fudge to celebrate! I told you I had my chafing-dish; don't you girls feel fudgy?"

"I could nibble a morsel," Bernice said, "and not half try. How about you, Dot?"

"I'm right there — with bells on!"

"Isn't it too late?" objected Dolly.

"Now, look here, priggy-wig," and Alicia shook a finger at her, "if you don't quit that spoilsporting of yours, there'll be trouble in camp! The truth is, there's not much fun in making fudge, just 'cause there's nobody to forbid it! At school, we have to do it on the sly. Here, if Mrs. Berry or Uncle Jeff knew we thought of it, they'd send forty 'leven footmen and maids to help us!"

"That's so," laughed Dolly; "I wasn't thinking of them. But isn't it time we all went to bed?"

"Of course it is, young hayseed. That's why we're staying up. Also, it makes you so delightfully sleepy next morning! Now, do you come to this fudge party or do you go to bed?"

"Do I come to it!" cried Dolly, in disdain. "Well, I like that! Why, your old fudge party is *for* me! I'm the heroine of the hour! Who went on your desperate and dangerous errand, I'd like to know! Who got permission to invite your old Coriell man to tea? Come, now, declare the fudge party a feast in my honour, or call it off!"

"It is! it is!" laughed Alicia. "To the victor belong the spoils. The party is *all* for you, and if you will accept our humble invitation come right into our room and make yourself at home."

So the two D's went into the other girls' room, and Alicia got out her chafing-dish set and prepared for the feast.

"How are you going to make fudge with nothing but chocolate?" laughed Dotty.

"That's so," said Alicia, looking blank. "I forgot I had to have milk and butter and sugar and a lot of things. Guess we can't do it."

"Guess we can!" retorted Bernice, and she pushed a bell button.

"Oh, Bernie!" exclaimed Dotty, "you oughtn't to call the maid so late! She'll be in bed."

"Then she won't answer," said Bernice, calmly.

But in a moment a maid did come, and smilingly listened to their requests.

" Some milk, please," said Alicia, " and sugar, and butter,—"

" All the things for fudge, miss? " asked the girl, her eyes taking in the chafing-dish. " Certainly. In a moment."

She disappeared and the girls burst into peals of laughter.

" It's impossible to do anything frisky here," said Alicia, " because everything we want to do, is looked on as all right ! "

" Well, it isn't a dreadful thing to make fudge of an evening," put in Bernice.

" No," agreed Dolly, " but I wouldn't think of doing it at my house. After I'd gone to my room for the night, I mean."

" It's a funny thing," said Alicia, " but all the fun of it's gone now. I don't care two cents for the fudge, it's the excitement of doing it secretly, that appeals to me. We do it at school, and we have to be so fearfully careful lest the teachers hear us."

" I know what you mean," said Dolly, " but I don't believe I feel that way. I love fudge, but I'd a whole lot rather have people know we're making it than to do it on the sly."

"You're a little puritan," and Alicia flew over and kissed her. "No wonder Mrs. Berry said yes to you, you probably made her think it was a duty to humanity!"

When the maid returned with the trayful of things they had asked for, there was also a goodly plate of frosted cakes and a dish of fruit.

"In case you might feel hungry," she explained. "Mrs. Berry was saying the other day, how hungry young folks do be gettin'. Shall I return for the tray, miss?"

"No," said Dolly, kindly. "You go to bed. We'll set the things out in the hall, when we're finished, and you can take them away in the morning."

"Thank you, miss," and the maid went away, leaving the girls to their spread.

"I'm not going to make fudge," said Alicia, "there's enough here to eat, without it."

"I'll do it, then," said Dolly. "I'm not going to make all this trouble and then not seem to appreciate it."

She began to cut the chocolate, and Dotty helped her.

Alicia made the chafing-dish ready, and Bernice set out a table for them.

"This is splendid fudge," Alicia remarked, as at last they sat enjoying the feast. "You must give me your recipe."

"Probably just like yours," smiled Dolly; "but it always tastes better if somebody else makes it."

"Not always! It depends on *who* makes it. This is fine!"

"Even if we are not doing it on the sly? I declare, Alicia, I can't understand that feeling of yours. I s'pose you don't care so much about Mr. Coriell, since Mrs. Berry is willing."

"It does take the snap out of it," Alicia admitted. "But I couldn't do that on the sly, anyway. I mean if I had him *here*. I wish I could meet him somewhere else,— at some tearoom, or somewhere."

"Oh, Alicia, I think you're horrid! Nice girls don't do things like that!" Dolly's big blue eyes expressed such amazement that Alicia laughed outright.

"You little innocent!" she cried.

"I'd rather be innocent than illbred," Dolly flashed back.

"Well, wait till you go to boarding-school and you'll get some of those strait-laced notions knocked out of you."

"I don't ever expect to go. I wouldn't like to leave home. And that reminds me, girls, I must skip. I've got to write up my diary before I go to bed. You do my share of the clearing up, won't you, Dot?"

"'Course I will," and Dolly ran off to the other room while the three cleared away the party and set the tray out in the hall.

"Is Dolly always so goody-goody?" asked Alicia.

Dotty took the question seriously. "I shouldn't call her that," she said; "but she isn't very mischievous, and she's as honest as the day is long. She positively abhors deceit. And, somehow, Alicia, all the things that you think are fun, are the sort of things she doesn't stand for. That's all. Doll isn't a prig,— is she, Bernice?"

"No; she's as fond of fun as anybody. But Alicia rubs her the wrong way."

" I don't mean to. Only I don't see any harm in pranks that *she* thinks are fearful."

" Well, you ought to bless her for getting the Coriell matter fixed up. I don't believe Mrs. Berry would have done it for any of us. But when Dolly asked her, I s'pose she made it seem all right."

" It *is* all right," defended Alicia.

" Oh, I don't know," and Bernice looked doubtful. " I don't think the Fayres or Roses would like it much; I doubt if my dad would approve. But what Mrs. Berry says, goes."

" It does *so!* " assented Alicia, and then they all said good-night.

Alicia's letter was mailed next morning and to her surprise a reply arrived about noon, brought by a messenger. It said:

My dear Miss Steele:

Your welcome invitation is here. I cannot accept for to-morrow as I have an important engagement then, but I will do myself the pleasure of calling upon you *to-day* at four o'clock, and trust I may find you at home.

Sincerely yours,

BAYNE CORIELL.

"Oh, isn't it wonderful!" sighed Alicia. "A letter from *him!* Oh, girls, I'm *so* happy! How *can* I wait for four o'clock!"

She ran away to tell Mrs. Berry of the letter.

"Very well," said the kind-hearted woman, "it's just as well to have him come to-day. Suppose we have tea in the small reception room, it's cosier than the drawing-room."

"All right," said Alicia. "Will Uncle Jeff come down, do you think?"

"I doubt it. However, I'll tell him you expect Mr. Coriell, and he can do as he likes." Mrs. Berry had a peculiar twinkle in her eye, and Alicia noted it, and wondered what it meant. The whole affair seemed mysterious, for she had not supposed Mrs. Berry would be so ready to receive this strange young man.

"You think it's all right for us to receive him, don't you, Mrs. Berry?" she asked, for she began to fear lest she had been too unconventional.

"I daresay it's all right, my dear. Of course, such things weren't done in my day, but young folks are different now. And Mr. Forbes said you girls were to do pretty much as you like."

"Were you surprised at our asking for this?" Alicia persisted.

"Well, yes, since you ask me, I must say I was surprised. Especially when I found Dolly Fayre was the ringleader."

"Oh,— well,— she *did* ask you, didn't she? Maybe Dolly isn't such a quiet little mouse as she seems."

"Dolly's all right," and Mrs. Berry spoke with some asperity. "Now, I'll send tea in at quarter past four, is that your idea?"

"Oh, Mrs. Berry, won't you be present?"

"No; I have my duties, and I observe them properly, but to preside at tea is not one of them. Your uncle expressly ordered that."

"Do you mean Uncle Jeff ordered that we should receive Mr. Coriell alone?"

"Well, he didn't direct that *I* should be there. If *he* wants to come down, he will."

"Very well," and Alicia suddenly became dignified, "we can manage. I suppose it will be proper to dress up a good deal?"

Again that amused smile flitted over Mrs. Berry's face.

" As you like," she said, indifferently. " All your frocks are pretty."

Alicia returned to the others, and told them all the conversation.

" I hope Uncle Forbes does come down," said Dolly, " I think it would be nicer to have him there."

" Come, now, old mother Prim, don't throw cold water on our little party," said Alicia. " You know how the conversation would run, with uncle at the helm ! "

" It wouldn't run at all," laughed Bernice, " it would stagnate ! "

When the girls began to dress for the tea, there was a wide diversity of opinion as to appropriate costumes.

" Our very best," said Alicia decidedly. " Nothing's too good for Bayne ! "

" You'd better be careful," warned Dotty, " you'll call him Bayne to his face ! You use it so much ! "

" Don't care if I do ! " returned Alicia, pertly. " I say, Doll, is *that* your best frock ? "

" Yes, except an evening one."

" Let's see your evening one. I'll bet it's just about right for this afternoon."

Dolly produced a pretty light blue affair of chiffon, and Alicia exclaimed, " Wear that, of course. It's really no evening dress at all, but it's a very nice afternoon thing."

Dolly looked dubious. " What are you going to wear, Dots? " she said.

" Oh, I s'pose we might as well wear our best ones. As Alicia says, they're all right for afternoon here, though they wouldn't be in Berwick."

" All right," and Dolly put on her pretty fluffy dress. Very lovely she looked, her golden curls twisted up high on her head, and held by a bandeau of blue ribbon.

Dotty's dress was yellow, and very becoming. She wore a black velvet headband, and Alicia cried out in approval when she saw the two D's ready for inspection.

" My! " she said, " you look better than I do! Now, I am mad! "

But her rage was only simulated, and she didn't really think what she said.

She herself wore a most elaborate embroidered dress of rich pink silk. It was trimmed, too, with pearl bead fringe, and to Dolly's simple taste it was too fussy. But Dotty admired it, and Bernice thought it wonderful.

"It *is* a good thing," said Alicia, carelessly. "It's imported. I've never had it on before."

Bernice had a lovely dress of white tulle, with white satin ribbons; — lovely, that is, for evening, but too dressy for daytime. However, as the winter dusk fell early, the lights were on, and it seemed almost like evening.

CHAPTER VIII

THE CALLER

THE four girls, in the reception room, waited the coming of their guest. To their surprise, Mr. Forbes came in, and looked them over with a chuckle.

"Well, you *are* ready for the fray, aren't you?" he said, taking in their dressy finery and their important, self-conscious airs.

"Yes, Uncle Jeff," responded Alicia; "will you stay and see our young man?"

For some unexplained reason, Uncle Jeff laughed heartily. But he checked his merriment, and said, "No, Alicia, I fear I might intrude; I know you want to flirt with this young actor, and I'd be a spoilsport. But let me warn you to be very gentle with him. You see, he may be so overcome by this galaxy of youth and beauty that he'll be embarrassed and run away!"

"Nonsense, uncle," said Bernice, " actors are not

-〔106〕-

easily embarrassed. More likely we girls will be struck dumb at his splendour and importance."

"Well, tell me all about it afterward," and still chuckling, Mr. Forbes went off.

"What ails Uncle?" said Alicia, pettishly. "Anybody'd think he had a joke on us."

"No," Dotty rejoined, "only he's sort of old, you know, and he doesn't see the fun in this, as we do."

"Well, I wish the fun would hurry up! It's after four now."

"Such people are never on time," said Alicia, with a great air of experience. "He's sure to be late. Oh, there's the bell now!"

The girls, with hearts beating high, grouped themselves in a picturesque pose, which they had practised beforehand, and breathlessly watched the doorway.

Through it came, in a moment, a jolly-faced man, with an informal manner and pleasant smile.

"Hullo, girlies," he said, "what's up? Expecting a party? Well, I won't keep you a minute. Where's Mr. Forbes?"

"Why, you're the party, Mr. Coriell," said Alicia,

stepping forward to greet him, and looking very coquettish as she smiled up into his face.

"Oh, am I! all right, have it your own way, kiddies. But I can't give you more than ten minutes of my valuable time. What do you want? Autographs? Or tickets for a box? Speak up, now."

"Oh, no!" exclaimed Bernice, for Alicia was speechless with disappointment at this prosaic attitude on the part of the visitor. "We just want to — to talk to you."

"You see," said Dolly, frankly, "we thought you'd be — different."

"Oh, of course you did! They always do! You wanted to see the Lascar, not plain James Brown!"

"What!" cried Alicia, hope rising in her breast that this was not the great actor after all, "aren't you Bayne Coriell?"

"Sure! That's my stage name, but in private life I'm James Brown, at your service."

"You don't even look like the Lascar!" wailed Dotty, dismayed at the turn things had taken.

"Of course, I don't, little one. Actors on and off, are two different persons. Oh, I begin to see

-⟨108⟩-

through this performance. Your uncle didn't tell you anything about me! Eh?"

"No, sir," said Dolly, as the others were silent. "We saw you in your play, and we admired your work so much, that we — we —"

"Oh, the matinée idol business! Well, well! I didn't expect that. Why, kiddies, outside the theatre, I'm just a plain United States citizen. I have a daughter about the age of you girls. My Muriel is fourteen, nearly fifteen, but she's taller than any of you. Your uncle is a great friend of mine. He was my father's chum, and he has been more than kind to me all my life. I supposed he knew all about the letter from Miss Alicia, and ran around here expecting to see you and him both."

"That's why he chuckled at us!" and Dolly's eyes twinkled at the joke. Somehow, she seemed more at ease with the actor than the other girls. "You see, Mr. Brown, we thought you'd be more like you are on the stage. Of course we didn't expect you'd be dressed like the Lascar, or — or — made up,— isn't that what you call it? but we thought you'd be stagy and actory —"

James Brown laughed. " Everybody thinks that, or something like it," he said. " Few people realise that an actor's profession is *merely* a profession,— a business; and that we discard it out of business hours."

" But don't you get lots of notes from — from your audiences? " asked Dotty.

" Indeed I do. My wife looks after 'em, and most of 'em go into the trash basket. But of course a note from Jefferson Forbes' home was welcome, and I was glad to call on his nieces. Are you all his nieces? "

" No," said Alicia, who had recovered her poise, and she introduced the other girls by name. " I wrote the note, because I thought you were —"

" Because you thought I was a gay young sport," laughed James Brown; " well, I'm sorry, for your sake, that I'm merely an uninteresting, middle-aged man, but, I doubt if your uncle would have let you send that note, if I had been a stranger to him. Take my advice, girls, for I know what I'm talking about, never write to an actor with whom you are not acquainted. It can never lead to any good result and might lead to great harm."

" Are they all bad? " asked Dolly, innocently.

" No, indeed, far from it. But many of them are thoughtless; and, too, if a girl so far forgets the conventions as to write to a stranger, an actor often thinks he is justified in meeting her half way. And nice girls don't write to men they don't know. The fact that a man is an actor, is no more reason to treat him informally than if he were a broker or a merchant. It is the glamour of the stage that blinds you to the proprieties. That's only natural, I know, and that's why I'm presuming to give you this little talk for your own good. If ever you feel moved to make advances to a matinée idol,— don't do it! "

Alicia looked decidedly chagrined and a little angry, but Mr. Brown proceeded to talk of other matters, and though it was plain to be seen he meant the advice he had given them, all unpleasant effect was forgotten as he began to tell them some funny anecdotes.

And then tea was brought in, and they all grouped round the teatable, still listening to his entertaining chat.

The actor was a good-looking man, but far from

being as handsome as he appeared on the stage. His fascination and charm were evidently as much put on as his swarthy complexion and long black hair, which so became him as an East Indian. Really, his hair was ash-coloured, and he was rather bald.

"I expect to go on the stage," observed Dolly, as they ate the cakes and bon-bons that accompanied the elaborate tea service.

"You do!" exclaimed the guest. "Why?"

"Because I feel I have talent for it. Not so much as an actress, perhaps, but as a singer. What shall I do first, Mr. Brown, to prepare for the light opera stage?"

James Brown looked at her kindly. "I see you are in earnest," he said, in a serious tone, "and so, I will treat your question practically. The first thing to do, is to finish your education, and then start on a course of voice training. By the time you have done these things, come to me again, and I will advise you further. Do you think me flippant?" he continued, as Dolly looked decidedly disappointed. "I am telling you just the line to follow that I expect my own daughter to pursue. Muriel has promise of a good singing voice. I assume you have that hope also, otherwise you wouldn't think of a stage career. Tell your parents what I have told you, and if they care to consult me on the subject I shall be more than glad to meet them."

"Good gracious! What a come down!" cried Dotty. "We thought of course Doll could start in in the chorus at most any time, and work up."

"That has been done successfully," and Mr. Brown smiled, "about one time in ten thousand. My plan is surer and better in every way."

"Is that the way Miss Marie Desmond learned?" asked Dolly, wistfully.

"Yes, my child. Miss Desmond worked long and faithfully before she attained her present position. If you'd care to meet her and have a little talk with her, I can arrange it. Suppose you all come to my house some afternoon, and Muriel will make a little party for you, and I'm sure I can persuade Miss Desmond to meet you for a few minutes at least. She is not a lady easy of access, I can tell you, but she will meet friends of mine."

"Well, well, Jim, hobnobbing with young people, are you?" sang out a hearty voice from the hall, and Uncle Jeff came stalking into the room. "Glad to see you, my boy. You seem to be getting on famously."

" Yes, indeed. Your nieces and their friends are the most charming bunch of young people I've seen in a long time. We're discussing all sorts of matters of interest. Join us in a cup of tea, won't you? "

" That's what I'm here for," and Uncle Jeff took a seat among the group. " Yes, thank you, Alicia, fix me up a cup. Sugar, please, but no lemon. How's your wife, Jim? Muriel all right? "

" Yes, thank you. I'm just asking these girls to come round, say to-morrow, for a little party. Or would you rather have a box party at the the-atre? "

The girls decided in favour of the afternoon party at Mr. Brown's home, and the matter was settled. And then, somehow, the two men fell into conversa-tion, which in no way interested the girls, being about political matters and business affairs. Indeed, their very presence seemed to be forgotten by the gentle-men. Absent-mindedly Uncle Jeff accepted a second cup of tea, and then a third, still arguing a point of finance with his guest.

Alicia, in high dudgeon, made a motion to the

others that they leave the room, and Dolly nodded assent.

So, noiselessly, the four rose from their seats, and stole out into the hall. Mr. Brown looked up, saw them go, and waved his hand with a smile of farewell, but Uncle Jeff paid no attention, if indeed, he noticed their departure.

" Well! of all things! " exclaimed Alicia, as they sought refuge in the library, which was in the rear of the house. " I call that positively insulting! "

" Now, 'Licia," and Dotty laughed, " you know the man said he could only give us ten minutes of his time, and he gave us more than a half hour. I don't think we've any reason to complain."

" Well, I do! It was a perfect fizzle, the whole thing! I'm utterly disgusted! Matinée idol! Pooh, he's just an every-day man! "

" Well, that's just what he said he was," rejoined Bernice, who was almost as much disappointed as Alicia. " But he was very kind and pleasant, I think."

" Oh, kind enough," and Alicia still pouted; " but I thought he would be young and — and sporty, you know."

"He certainly isn't sporty! whatever he is," said Dolly. "I think he's awfully nice. I'm glad we're going to his daughter's party. It's fine to go to a place like that."

"She's just a little girl," complained Alicia. "Fourteen years old! I don't want to go to an infant class!"

"All right," put in Bernice, "you can stay home then. I'm delighted to go. To think of telling the girls at home that we went to Bayne Coriell's daughter's party! My, won't they think we're grand!"

"That's so," agreed Alicia. "Not everybody could get such an invitation. We couldn't, only that he's Uncle Jeff's friend. But I can tell you, girls, if I hadn't got up this whole scheme we wouldn't have been asked there. You can thank me for it."

"Dolly, too," said Dotty. "If she hadn't asked Mrs. Berry, he wouldn't have come at all."

"Yes, he would; why wouldn't he?"

"Oh, pshaw! It was all made up by Uncle Jeff. You could see that. Mrs. Berry told him, and he let us go ahead, just to have a joke on us. Mr. Brown came mostly to see Mr. Forbes,— not us."

"You're right, you little smarty-cat," and Alicia

smiled at the astute Dotty. " And I do believe Uncle Jeff meant to give us a lesson about writing to actors. I thought it was queer he took it so easily, — and Mrs. Berry too. They played right into our hands. They wouldn't have done that if the actor person had been a stranger."

" Of course they wouldn't," and Dotty wagged her head. " I felt sure there was some reason why Mrs. Berry said yes to Doll so easily. But I didn't think Coriell Bayne, or whatever his name is, was old enough to be Uncle Forbes' chum."

" He isn't exactly," said Dolly; " that is, he said his father and Mr. Forbes were friends. I suppose the son carried on the friendship."

" He looks as old as my father,— off the stage," said Bernice; " but on it, he might be my father's son!"

" You can't tell a thing about actors!" declared Alicia. " If ever I think another one is handsome and fascinating, I'll remember James Bayne, and know he's nothing but an old fogy!"

" Oh, I don't call Mr. Brown an old fogy," defended Dotty. " I think he's interesting and pleasant; just about like my father, or yours, Doll."

"He's not a bit like our fathers, though he doesn't look much younger. Anyway, I'm glad I've met him, but he did give me a setback about my career."

"Is that a real stunt, Dolly?" and Alicia looked at her curiously. "Do you really want to go on the stage? It doesn't seem like you."

"Yes, I do, or at least, I did, until Mr. Brown said what he did. I don't know as I want to devote my whole life to getting ready for a stage career. I'm going to think it over and see about it."

"You funny little thing! I hope you'll decide to do it, and in about ten or twenty years, when I'm an old married woman, I'll come to your first performance."

"Whose performance? Who's stage struck?" asked Uncle Jeff, walking in at the door. He had a way of appearing unexpectedly.

"Dolly," answered Alicia. "She wants to be a prima donna."

"Bless my soul!" exclaimed the old man, "why, one reason I had Jim Brown here to-day, was to knock such foolishness out of your heads."

"And he did his part all right, Uncle Forbes,"

said Dolly, looking serious, " but I don't quite take the knocking. At least, I haven't decided what I'll do about it."

" Oho, you haven't, haven't you? " and the old man raised his shaggy eyebrows. " Well, Alicia, how did you like your handsome, fascinating, young man? "

Alicia had quite recovered her good humour, and she replied, laughingly, " Oh, except that he isn't very young or handsome or fascinating, I liked him pretty well."

" You're a good girl," pronounced her uncle. " I thought maybe you'd resent the little trick I played on you. But when you raved over the handsome hero, and the Greek god effects of him, I couldn't refrain from showing you how deceitful appearances may be. Jim's a fine chap, not at all a silly flirt, and his daughter is a lovely young girl, a little older than you girls —"

" Why, Uncle Jeff, Mr. Brown says she's younger, he said Muriel is not yet fifteen."

" Bless me! is that so? Well, he must know. But I can tell you, she seems as old or older than any of you. I suppose because she's been brought up among stage people. But a mighty nice girl, all the same. And Mrs. Brown is a delightful woman. All nice people. I'm glad he asked you to his home. It'll be a rare treat for you."

"When is it to be, to-morrow?" asked Dotty.

"We don't know yet. When Brown went away he said he'd consult his wife and daughter and telephone us about it. I fancy they'll make quite an affair of it. See here, have you all proper frocks to wear? I don't want my girls less well dressed than the others there. And I have a sneaking notion these are your best clothes." Uncle Jeff's eyes twinkled as he glanced at their dresses. "Anyway, I'd like to give each of you a new frock. Go to-morrow morning and get them."

And having given the order, Uncle Jeff stalked away.

CHAPTER IX

FINE FEATHERS

"ISN'T he the funniest and the very dearest old thing in the world!" said Alicia, in a whisper, as Mr. Forbes disappeared. "I've got loads of clothes, but I'm glad to have him give me a dress, for I'll warrant it'll be about the best money can buy."

"Let's get the best New York can show us," chimed in Bernice.

"I can't do it," said Dolly, decidedly. "My mother wouldn't like me to accept a dress from Mr. Forbes."

"Oh, fiddlesticks, Dollyrinda!" said Dotty, "it's not charity. My mother wouldn't let me either, ordinarily speaking, but this is different."

"How is it different?"

"Why, Mr. Forbes doesn't look on it as giving us clothes because we're poor —"

"He does so, Dot! You can't fool me! He knows that Alicia and Bernie can afford grand clothes and we can't, and so he gives us each a dress to make it easy for us to take them."

Now, Alicia privately thought this was just about the truth, but Bernice thought differently; "Rubbish!" she cried. "Uncle Jeff doesn't think anything of the sort! He's so kind-hearted, he wants us all to have things nice, and he doesn't even think about whether it would hurt our feelings or not. Why, Dolly, the price of a dress is no more to him, than a glass of soda water would be to us."

"I know that's so," and Dolly's blue eyes looked very troubled, "but it isn't nice to take clothing from anybody but your own people."

"But Dolly," argued Alicia, "if you kick up a bobbery, and refuse to take this kind offer, then we'll all have to do the same, and you deprive us all of the pretty presents."

"Oh, Alicia, I'd be sorry to do that!"

"Well, that's what it would amount to. Now, be sensible, and go with us to-morrow, and we'll all get lovely dresses, and it will please Uncle Jeff. I know he'd be hurt and offended, if you refused, Dolly."

"I'll see about it; I'll think it over," and that was all Dolly would say about it then.

But next morning, Mrs. Berry informed them that they were asked to an At Home at Mrs. Brown's that afternoon, from four till seven, and she further said that of her knowledge, it would be an occasion where the nicest possible apparel would be required.

"Gorgeous!" cried Alicia; "Uncle Jeff told us yesterday, we could get new frocks as presents from him. We can get them at Follansbee's, and if they need alteration, they'll do it for us at once, as the case is so especial."

Dolly's objections were overruled, even Mrs. Berry siding with the other girls.

"Yes, indeed, Dolly," she said; "you will spoil the pleasure of the others if you refuse to do as they do. And it would grieve Mr. Forbes if he thought you didn't appreciate or accept his kind offer. Run along, girls, all of you, and get your hats and coats, the car will be here in a few minutes."

"Won't you go with us, Mrs. Berry," asked Dolly, "to help pick them out? We don't know about these things as well as some one who lives in the city."

" No, dearies. But you won't have any trouble. Just ask for Mrs. Baxter at Follansbee's and her judgment will be the right thing. Be sure to take what she advises. She'll know."

In gay spirits the quartette started off, Dolly joining in the general enthusiasm, for having decided to do as the others did, she had no wish to hesitate further.

Mrs. Baxter was more than pleased to advise and suggest to Jefferson Forbes' relatives, and she had her assistants bring out dozens of frocks for inspection.

At last, after much discussion and trying on, the four were selected and were promised for two o'clock that afternoon. What slight alterations were necessary could be done in that time, and there would be no doubt of prompt delivery.

The dresses were absolutely unlike any the girls had ever owned before. They were all imported models, and though of finest materials, were simple in fabric and design. Yet they had an air and an effect never achieved by a village dressmaker or a department store.

Dolly's was of fine white net, frilled with delicate

lace, and adorned with tiny rosebud garlands, and knots of pale blue velvet.

Dotty's, of apricot pink crêpe, with hints of silver lace peeping through its chiffon draperies. Alicia's was corn-coloured crêpe de chine with cherry velvet decorations, and Bernice rejoiced in a white embroidered net, made up over green silk.

All had that indefinable charm which betokens the genius of a great modiste, and the girls were enchanted with the wonderful robes.

"But what awful prices!" said Dolly, as they drove away from the shop. "I'm sure mother will be displeased. I feel awfully about it."

"Now, Doll," said Dotty, sensibly, "you can't help it now. So don't let it spoil your pleasure and ours too. When we get home you can tell your mother just how it was. I'll tell her too, and I'm sure she'll see that you couldn't do anything else than get the frock, or kick up a terrible bobbery!"

This was common sense, as Dotty's remarks often were, so Dolly accepted the situation, and made the best of it.

And that afternoon, when they were all arrayed in the new frocks, and presented themselves to Uncle

Jeff for inspection, his approval was so hearty, that Dolly was very glad she hadn't put a damper on the whole thing by remaining obstinate.

"You are visions of beauty," he declared, as he looked at each in turn. "Madame Who-ever-it-was, turned you out remarkably well. I don't know much about feminine millinery, but I've a general idea of the fitness of things. And I'll bet a thousand dollars that these affairs are in better taste than the rigs you had on yesterday, though those were far gayer."

"You do know a lot about it, Uncle," said Bernice. "These are way ahead of our best dresses, but it's because they came from a high class shop. And when you get the bill you'll open your eyes!"

"That's all right, Bernie. I'm an old bachelor, you know, and never before have I had the privilege of buying dresses for anybody. I'm downright glad if you girls are pleased with these, and I'm downright proud of the little cavalcade setting forth from my house."

The courteous old gentleman made a profound bow and the girls curtseyed in response. Then off they went to the party.

-⟨126⟩-

As Mrs. Berry had foretold, fine clothes were the order of the day at the Brown house. Everything was as formal as a grown-up affair. The girls were ushered to a dressing-room to take off their wraps, and then at the drawing-room door, their names were announced by an imposing-looking personage in livery, and they were swept along into the room, by the crush of others behind them.

Mrs. Brown and her daughter were receiving, and they greeted each arrival with gay banter and smiles.

"Ah, my dears, how do you do?" said Mrs. Brown to our girls. "I am so glad to welcome Mr. Forbes' young people. Muriel, dear, these are the girls daddy told you about last night. 'Member?"

"'Course I do. Aw'fly jolly to have you here. Sweet of you to come. Wish I could chin-chin more, but I'll see you after the rush is over."

They passed in line, saying scarce a word beyond a mere greeting, and following the example of their predecessors they took seats in what seemed to be a large auditorium. A curtained stage faced them, and they looked about at the fast gathering audience. It was a merry crowd of young people all

laughing and chattering, and all arrayed in beautiful clothes after the order of those the girls wore
themselves. There were many boys present, too,
and they moved easily about, joking with their
friends here and there. Presently two boys drifted
toward our quartette, and one of them said, "What'll
be the show, do you know?"

"No," said Dotty, her black eyes dancing with
the excitement of the scene; "what do you guess?"

"Dunno. Last time they had minstrels, and the
time before, a magicker."

"Legerdemain?"

"Yes; rabbits out of hats, and that sort. Can't
we sit here? Engaged?"

"No," and Dotty smiled as she looked toward the
other girls for their consent.

"Oh, let us stay," said the other boy, in a wheedling voice. "We'll be awfully good,— so good you
won't know us."

"We don't know you, anyway," laughed Alicia,
and the first boy responded, "Sure enough. Roof's
the introduction, you know, but I'll add that this
marvellously handsome companion of mine is one

Geordie Knapp, and I'm Ted Hosmer, very much at your service."

"Well," said Alicia, "we're Miss Forbes, Miss Fayre, Miss Rose and Miss Steele. Shall I tell you which is which, or let you guess?"

"Let us Sherlock it out!" exclaimed Geordie Knapp. "I know you're Miss Steele because you mentioned yourself last."

"Right!" and Dotty clapped her hands in admiration of his quickness. "Now, which am I?"

"Rosy Posy!" declared Ted Hosmer, little thinking he had guessed correctly, but saying so because of Dotty's pink cheeks.

"Yes, sir! you *are* a Sherlock Holmes. Now which is Miss Forbes?"

"I'm not going to guess any more, I'll spoil my record," and Ted looked uncertainly from Dolly to Bernice. "But as you two are named Forbes and Fayre, I'll call you both Miss F., and so be sure of you."

And then the curtain began to rise, and the young people became silent.

The entertainment was very amusing, being entirely in pantomime, and performed by exceedingly clever actors.

The story depicted was funny, and the antics of the performers were novel and humorous, and the room resounded with laughter from the appreciative audience. There were about a hundred young people present yet the large room was only partly filled. Dolly concluded, as she looked about, that it was a sort of small theatre where Mr. Brown rehearsed his own plays. In this she was partly right, although it had been built more for entertainment of the actor's guests. James Brown, or Bayne Coriell, as he was more often called, stood very high in his profession, and had hosts of friends and acquaintances. His wife was popular, too, and Muriel was just beginning to take her place in society.

After the pantomime was over, two celebrated dancers gave an exhibition of their skill, and then Miss Marie Desmond appeared and sang two of her songs from " The Lass and the Lascar."

Dolly was enthralled. She sat, listening to every note, and admiring the graceful manner and deportment of Miss Desmond as well as enjoying her music.

" Well, you seemed to care for that, Miss F.,"

said Ted Hosmer. "You didn't move an eyelash while Marie was on!"

"Oh, I did enjoy it!" and Dolly's eyes shone with delight. "Isn't she a splendid singer!"

"Top notch! I like her lots. Hello, here's our charming hostess."

The programme was over now, and Muriel Brown sought out the Forbes party to invite them to the refreshment room.

"I feel that I know you," she laughed, "from Dad's description. He says the fair girl is Miss Fayre, and the rosy girl, Miss Rose."

"Oh, that's it, is it?" cried Ted; "then this is Miss Forbes, and now all the problems are solved!" He looked at Bernice, who acknowledged the fact, and then Muriel was pounced upon by a rush of young people, and literally carried away.

"Great girl, Muriel," said young Hosmer. "Never saw such a favourite. I say, mayn't we take you girls to the supper room? Or don't you eat?"

"Indeed we do," said Alicia, laughing, "but I may as well own up I'm so interested in looking about me, I'm not conscious of hunger."

"Well, come ahead to the dining-room, and you can eat and look about at the same time. I'll corral a couple more henchmen to help in your services and we'll flock by ourselves."

Geordie whistled to a couple of his chums, whom he presented as Marly Turner and Sam Graves.

"Now," went on Geordie, who was a born manager, "we're eight of us,— that's enough for a table to our own selves. Nail one, Samivel."

The way to the dining-room lay through a crush of guests, every one, it seemed, headed in a different direction.

"Why don't they all go one way?" asked Dotty.

"Few of 'em eat," replied Ted. "Most of 'em going on. But the food's always fine here, and anyway you girls want to see the dining-room if you've never been here before. It's a whole show."

It was. The splendid great room, with vaulted ceiling, represented an old English hall. There was a raised platform across the end and a gallery on either side. Fine paintings and tapestries adorned the walls, and a multitude of small tables offered places for all who chose to sit at them.

"Here we are," and the boys decided on a table

in a desirable position, from which the girls could see the gay scene. " Now for some supper."

Obsequious waiters appeared and soon the party was served with viands fit for a king.

" Told you so," said Ted. " Trust the Coriell bunch to give you eats worth-while. Oh, I guess yes! "

" But it's getting so late," sighed Dolly, as she caught sight of an old English clock that hung near by. " And Mr. Brown promised me I could speak to Miss Desmond. I'm afraid she'll be gone."

" 'Fraid she's gone now," said Ted. " But I'll flee and discover."

He left them and threaded his way among the crowd.

" Here we are! " he cried gaily, as he returned, bringing the lady in question. " Just caught her on the fly. Trust little Teddums to get you what you want, Miss Fair Dolly."

Marie Desmond greeted the girls as Ted named them.

" You lovely kiddies! " she cried. " What a delectable bunch! I could eat you all up. And your frocks! Paris! I know; you needn't tell *me!* Are you all sisters? Oh, no, I remember now; you have variegated names. Which one of you wanted to talk to me? I've a whole minute to spare! Never say *I'm* not a lady of leisure!"

"I'm the one," said Dolly, her eyes fixed on the lovely, laughing face of the actress. "But a minute is no good, thank you. I want to talk to you about a whole day!"

"Oh, I *do* wish we could manage it," and Miss Desmond appeared to think that was the one thing on earth she desired. But Dolly noted her wandering attention, and was not surprised when she left them as suddenly as she had come, and with a fleeting, smiling good-bye.

"Oh, isn't she exquisite!" breathed Dolly, her eyes on the disappearing figure.

"You bet she is!" assented Marly Turner. "And it's a wonder she took a step out of her way to speak to us kids. But friends of Coriell,— of course."

"Is she so very busy?" asked Dolly her eyes wide with interest.

"Well, she's a society belle as well as a popular actress. So, I s'pose, she has more or less on all the time. There's no time for much of anything in New

York. I say, can't us fellows come to see you girls? When? Where?"

"I don't know," said Dolly, mindful of the Coriell episode. "I'm not going to say yes till I know what's right. I'll ask Uncle Forbes."

"Do. Here's a telephone call that'll reach us. Let us come soon." And then Mrs. Brown appeared, spoke a few words to the girls, and the boys with them, and in a moment everybody was going home. Our girls followed the example set them, said their good-byes, went to the cloak-room for their wraps, and bade the footman at the door call the Forbes car.

CHAPTER X

A SKATING PARTY

THAT evening, in the drawing-room, Mr. Forbes questioned the girls rather closely as to their enjoyment of the party at the Browns'.

"I liked it," said Dolly, "but it was queer,— that's what it was,— queer. The idea of just seeing a performance on the stage, and then rushing through a very fancy supper, and then scooting for home as if the house was on fire!— that's not my idea of a party!"

Uncle Jeff laughed. "And you, Dotty," he said, "how did it strike you?"

"I adored it! Everybody was so gay and smartly dressed and quick-spoken,— I do like to hear people say things fast."

"How queer you are!" exclaimed Bernice; "why do you like to hear people talk fast?"

"Not talk fast exactly, but say things suddenly, funny things, I mean."

-⟨136⟩-

"I understand," said Mr. Forbes; "you mean bright at repartee and quick-witted."

"Yes, sir, that's just what I do mean. And everything was so well planned and well arranged,— oh, I enjoyed every minute of it."

"Well, I didn't," said Bernice. "I'd rather go to a regular party, where they play games and dance and act sociable."

"Why, the people were sociable enough," put in Alicia. "I'm like Dot, I thought it was lovely! Muriel is as pretty as a picture —"

"She scarcely said three words to us!" complained Bernice.

"She couldn't help that. There were so many guests, that she hadn't time to more than speak a minute or two with each one of them."

"I like Berwick parties better," persisted Bernice. "There we all know each other —"

"But, Bernie," said Dolly, laughing, "all the people at this party knew each other,— nearly. We were strangers, of course, but the rest seemed to be well acquainted with Muriel."

"And I thought the party was to be for us," went on Bernice, "and I thought we'd be introduced to everybody, and be — well, be *somebody*, you know."

" Oho! you wanted to be honoured and lionised! " and Uncle Jeff's eyes twinkled.

" Not exactly. But I understood from Mr. Brown that the whole affair was gotten up for us, and so I think we ought to have been noticed more. Why, the boys just scraped acquaintance with us, and even had to ask our names! "

" That's the way they do at large parties, Bernie," said her uncle. " You are supposed to talk to any of the other guests without introduction."

" Well, it's no sort of a way! They were awfully nice boys, but I don't suppose we'll ever see them again."

" Oh, yes, we will," said Dolly. " They asked to call on us, and I said I'd ask you, Uncle Forbes. Would it be all right? "

" Bless my soul, Dolly! I don't know. I've so little knowledge of etiquette for young people. Ask Mrs. Berry, whatever she says, you may do. Who are the boys? Hosmer? Knapp? Oh, they're all right. I know the families. But as to their calling, put it up to Mrs. Berry. And, by the way, how'd you girls like to have a party, a real one? "

" Like the one we went to to-day? " asked Bernice, doubtfully. " I don't care much about it."

" Well, have some other kind. There must be other ways of entertaining. What would you like, Bernice? "

" I'd like a little party,— but I suppose that would have to be formal, too."

" Oh, gracious, you old hayseed! " exclaimed Alicia. " You go back to the country! I'd love to have a party, Uncle, the biggest and grandest there is! Muriel Brown would invite the people for us, I'm sure. Oh, it would be just heavenly! We'd have an orchestra, and a midnight supper, and — oh, and everything! "

" Hold on, my child, don't go too fast! We'll only have what you all agree on. Come, two D's, what do you say? "

" We oughtn't to say," laughed Dolly. " It's for your nieces to choose. And anyway, Dot and I like everything, and we'd enjoy any kind of a party — or no party at all."

" You've a nice disposition," said Mr. Forbes, looking at her. " Don't you ever lose your temper? "

" She hasn't any to lose! " Dotty answered for her.
" In fact, she's too awfully good-natured for any
use! But she has other faults. She's as stubborn
as a perfectly good mule! Aren't you, Dollums? "

" I s'pect I am," and the golden head nodded.
" But only when I care enough to be stubborn. As
to this party, I don't care what sort it is, 'cause I
know it will be lovely, anyway. That is, if we have
it. But seems to me invitations for a big affair
ought to be sent out several days in advance, and
we'll be going home the middle of next week."

" Why, you've only just got here! " said Mr.
Forbes.

" Well, it's Friday night now, and we came last
Wednesday for a week. So, if we go home next
Wednesday, that party would have to be in three or
four days, and that's a short time."

" Of course," agreed Alicia. " We couldn't give a
big party on such short notice."

" That's easily arranged," and Mr. Forbes
laughed; " stay another week."

" Oh, I couldn't," cried Dolly. " My mother
wouldn't hear of such a thing. The other girls can,
though."

"I wouldn't if Doll didn't," declared Dotty. "But Bernie and Alicia could stay."

"So we could," said Bernice. "My father will let me stay as long as Uncle Jeff wants me."

"I can stay, too," said Alicia. "But it's lots more fun to have you other girls with us."

"We'll see about all that," and Mr. Forbes dismissed the subject.

A footman came in to say that Miss Fayre was wanted on the telephone.

"Oh!" cried Dolly, her face turning white, "do you suppose anything's wrong at home? Mother had a cold; maybe it's developed into pneumonia!"

"Nonsense, child; don't borrow trouble. Probably it's nothing of the sort."

"Isn't that Dolly all over?" said Alicia, after Dolly had left the room. "She always thinks the worst there is to think!"

"Maybe she's right," said Dotty. "Mrs. Fayre does have awful colds,— hark, I hear Dolly laughing! It's all right!"

They all listened, and they heard Dolly say, "Oh, perfectly splendid! I'd just love it!— Thank you!— Yes, indeed!— I'm 'most sure—

oh, delightful! — Well, I'll ask her — Fine! — Yes, yes,— just wait a minute,— I'll ask her now — hold the wire."

Followed a whispered conversation, and the girls caught the sound of Mrs. Berry's voice.

Unable to restrain their curiosity longer, the three rushed out to the hall and saw Dolly, her hand over the transmitter, talking to Mrs. Berry.

"What is it? Tell us all!" cried Bernice, and Alicia crowded close to listen.

"Oh, girls," and Dolly beamed at them, "it's the loveliest invitation! Marly Turner wants us to go to a skating party to-morrow afternoon at St. Valentine's rink! And Mrs. Berry says it will be all right for us to go. Yes," she continued, speaking into the telephone. "Yes, we can go. And we're all most happy to accept. What time?"

"Four o'clock," came the answer. "Meet our crowd at the rink. So glad you can come."

"So are we," returned Dolly, "and thank you, ever so much. Good-bye."

"Good-bye," said Turner, and Dolly hung up the receiver.

"Tell us more," cried Alicia. "What did you

hang up so soon for? Why didn't you let *us* talk **to** him? What an old selfish you are!"

"I couldn't, Alicia," and Dolly looked hurt. "I knew from his manner and speech that he only wanted a reply to his invitation, and I wasn't expected to say more."

"But why did he ask for you?" grumbled Alicia; "why not for me?"

"I don't know, I'm sure," and Dolly laughed; "he did, that's all. Let's go and tell Uncle Forbes about it."

"All right, girls; all right. Glad you're going. Have a good time. Marly Turner? Yes, yes, son of the Bayard Turners. Nice boy. His crowd will be all right. Can you all skate? Did you bring your skates? If not, get some. Get whatever you want. Look as good as the rest. Good-night now. Good-night, all."

Abruptly, as usual, Mr. Forbes left the room, and as the girls were getting accustomed to his eccentricities they nodded their good-nights, and then began to plan for the skating party.

Mrs. Berry appeared and helped them decide on certain details of costume and accessories.

The two D's had brought the pretty skating costumes they had worn at the Berwick carnival, but as
Bernice had been the queen that night, her white
velvet gown was out of the question. Alicia, too,
had no appropriate garb, so these two bought new
dresses.

The final result was four very becomingly attired
girls who started merrily off on Saturday afternoon
for the party at the rink.

Four bunches of violets, with Marly Turner's
card, had come to the house, and each fair damsel
wore one at her corsage.

Dolly's suit was of light blue cloth trimmed with
silver fox, and Dotty's was red cloth with dark fur.

Bernice looked very handsome in white cloth, and
Alicia had chosen emerald green.

They were met at the rink by Marly and his
chums, and at once introduced to the chaperon of the
affair, who was Marly's married sister. She didn't
look much older than the boy himself, but she greeted
the girls with a charming hospitality and declared
herself delighted to take them in charge.

The other boys whom they had met at Muriel's
party were there, and Muriel was, too. She wel-

comed the four warmly, but as she was constantly in demand by other gay young friends, they had no chance for connected conversation with her.

Indeed, connected conversation was not thought of, unless with one's skating partner.

"You're all right on runners," commented Geordie Knapp, as he skated with **Dotty**. "You must be fond of it."

"Oh, I am. I skate a lot at home; that is, when there's ice. We're dependent on that, you see, as we haven't an ice rink in Berwick."

"Berwick? Small town?"

"Yes. 'Bout as big as a minute," and Dotty laughed good-naturedly.

"That's why you're so up to the minute, then," Geordie laughed back. "Want to sit down and rest a bit?"

"All right. Let's," and they sat down for a few moments.

"There goes your chum,— with Ted Hosmer. She is your chum, isn't she? The Fair Dolly?"

"Dolly Fayre? Yes, indeed; we're super-inseparable."

"That's the way with Ted and me. We're always

together. Funny, isn't it, how you like one person better'n anybody else?"

"Yes; I couldn't keep house without Dolly. And we do keep house!" and Dotty told her companion all about Treasure House and its delights.

"Wow! That's some stunt! A house like that! I'd like to see it."

"Do. Some day next summer come out to Berwick and I'll show it to you. We've great little old brothers, too. One apiece."

"Have you? I s'pose you can cut up larks in the country that you couldn't here?"

"It's awfully different." Dotty sighed. "I like the city better in lots of ways, but, altogether, I guess I'd rather live in Berwick."

"What are you two confabbing about?" sang out a voice, and Dolly, with Ted Hosmer, came gliding up and stopped in front of Dot and young Knapp.

"Settling the affairs of the nation," said Geordie; "also, it's a case of 'change partners.'" He jumped up, took Dolly's hands in his, and they swayed off across the ice, leaving Dotty and Ted together.

"Don't mind him; he's crazy," said Ted, as he dropped onto the seat beside Dotty. "And anyway, we're such chums we share our best friends with each other!"

"Glad you do! I like to talk to different people —"

"I'm a different people; oh, I assure you I am. Please like to talk to me!"

"I do. Or, at least, I'm sure I shall. What shall we talk about?"

"Sports in general. What do you like best, next to skating?"

"Tennis, don't you?"

"Sure, if you do. But that's mostly for summer. Come on, let's skate round a couple of times, and then go for the tea place."

It was good fun skating with Ted, and, as Dolly told him, he reminded her a little of her friend, Tad Brown.

"Any kin of Muriel's?"

"No, a boy in Berwick. He has a twin brother, Tod."

"Great names! Tadpole and Toddlekins, in full, I suppose."

"They are called those sometimes. Oh, Mrs. Graham is beckoning to us. We must go."

They joined Mrs. Graham, who was their chaperon, and she marshalled her crowd of young people to the tea room.

At last Muriel Brown found a chance to talk to our girls.

"We seem like old friends," she said, gaily. "Isn't the ice fine to-day? Are you going to the dance to-night? What? Not invited? That can easily be remedied. I say, Sam, don't you want these four angel children at your party?"

"'Deed I do!" and Sam Graves beamed broadly. "I didn't dare ask them myself,— meant to get you to do it. Coax 'em, Muriel. Make 'em say yes."

Alicia took it upon herself to accept this invitation, though Dolly insisted it would depend on Mrs. Berry's sanction.

"Who's Mrs. Berry?" asked Muriel. "Is she a dragon?"

"No, indeed," smiled Dotty; "she's the dearest old, yes — sayer in the world!"

"Oh, she'll let you come then. Tell the girls all about it, Sam," and Muriel moved away.

" She went off and left her ice cream untouched!"
exclaimed Dotty.

" She's always on the hop,— Muriel is," said Sam.
" Now you girls come to-night, won't you? It's a
small and early at my house. Mr. Forbes knows me,
and I know your Mrs. Berry, too. Just tell her it's
little Sammy's party, and she'll send you flying
over."

" Tell us something about it," said Dolly. " Is it
to be very grand? We're hazy on the subject of
New York dances."

" Can you dance?"

" Yes, though maybe not the very latest steps."

" That's all right, then. Put on a clean sash and
come along. You won't be wall flowers!"

" What time shall we come?" asked Bernice.
" Tell me about the details; I'm Mr. Forbe's niece."

Bernice was always a little jealous if the D's
seemed to be consulted rather than herself or Alicia.

" Oh, no details specially. All informal, you
know. Come when you like,— nine, maybe, or half
past. If you're feeling conventional about it, my
mother will call on you — by telephone — and ask
you proper."

"Oh, no, she needn't do that," and Bernice laughed at the idea. "We're only little girls. If Mrs. Berry says we can go, your invitation is enough."

"Good work! Be sure to come. Crazy to have you. 'Scuse me a minute,— there's a girl I want to speak to."

Sam darted off, and another boy dropped into his vacated seat. It was this touch and go effect that Dotty liked, but to Dolly it seemed a whirling maze.

And, indeed, almost before they knew it they were all whirled off home.

CHAPTER XI

THE COLLECTIONS

O N Sunday, dinner was in the middle of the day, and directly after it was over Mr. Forbes led the four to the drawing-room, as was usual in the evening, and asked an account of the dance.

"It was lovely!" vouchsafed Dotty.

"Gorgeous!" agreed Bernice.

"Perfectly all right," Alicia averred.

"Nice enough, but very grown uppish," was Dolly's verdict.

"You stick to your taste for simpler parties?" said Mr. Forbes, looking kindly at Dolly.

"Yes, sir; I guess I'm a country girl."

"Well, I'm not," and Dotty's black eyes flashed. "I'd just as lief live in Berwick, to be sure; but I do love to visit in New York and see all the grand doings."

"And was the party grand?"

"Oh, it was, uncle," said Alicia. "It was small and it was early."

"Pooh!" cried Dolly. "We came home at half past eleven. I don't call that early!"

"Early for a city party," insisted Alicia, "but it was an elaborate affair, after all, and what do you s'pose, Uncle Jeff? We had invitations to a lot of things, next week and the week after, too."

"Well, you girls are real belles!"

"They do seem to like us," and Alicia looked very well self-satisfied.

"Which one of you do they like the best?" teased Uncle Jeff.

"Dotty," said Alicia and Bernice together.

"Nothing of the sort!" declared Dotty, blushing rosy red.

"Who, then?" and Mr. Forbes turned to her.

"Why, I don't know," said Dotty, still embarrassed. "Dolly, I guess."

"You know better, Dot," and Dolly laughed at her. "I think, Uncle Forbes, the most citified boys and girls like Bernie and Alicia best, and some of the others take to Dot and me."

Her honest blue eyes proved this was her true opinion, whatever the facts might be.

"Well, look here," and Mr. Forbes' eyes twinkled,

"I ask you two, Dotty and Dolly, which of my two nieces is a greater favourite?"

"Why, how can we tell that, right before them both?" cried Dolly, taking it as a joke.

"Yes, I want you to tell me,— right before them."

"I don't think there's a bit of difference," Dotty said, speaking seriously, and looking at the two girls. "You see, everybody likes Bernie — and — they all like Alicia."

"You're a diplomat!" laughed the old man. "Now, Dolly, see if you can beat that?"

Dolly liked being put on her mettle, and after a moment's thought, when she pretended to study the girls, she said, "They are both liked tremendously for themselves,— but more, because they are your nieces."

"Capital!" and Mr. Forbes rubbed his hands in glee. "You're a tactful young person, I do avow. Now, just for that you may ask anything of me you like, to the half of my kingdom."

"I'll ask," said Dolly, quickly, "before you have a chance to repent of that offer. This is what I want: Let us go up and see your collections. May we?"

"I s'pose so. Will you be good little girls, and not finger the exhibits, except such as I say you may?"

"Of course we will. We're not mischievous little kiddies! Oh, are you really going to let us see it! When?"

"Now. May as well get it over, I suppose. March!"

He led the way, and the girls trooped after him, up to the fourth floor of the house.

The rooms corresponded to those below stairs, but all were arranged as a museum. There were enormous cases filled with specimens of every sort of bird, butterfly or insect. Or, if not every kind was represented, surely they were nearly all there, so multitudinous were the exhibits.

"What a lot!" exclaimed Dolly. "I had no idea it was such an enormous collection."

"Yes," said Mr. Forbes, with justifiable pride, " it is the largest private collection that I know of. Come, let me show you the birds first."

Obediently the girls followed his directions, and with ever growing interest they saw the rows and rows of stuffed birds, of all sizes and of all varieties of plumage.

Then came great cabinets filled with shallow drawers, each of which, when opened, displayed tiny moths, queer flies, and microscopic insects, each daintily mounted on its own pin and all standing in trim rows.

The butterflies were the prettiest exhibit of all. These showed rare varieties and well-known ones; specimens from far distant countries and from their own state.

All the girls were interested, but Dolly was absorbed. She walked from case to case, asking intelligent questions, that Mr. Forbes was glad to answer.

"You ought to make natural history a special study," he said to her. "You seem so fond of it."

"Oh, I am!" responded Dolly. "I shall try to get mother to let me take it up specially next year. And here are the beetles! How wonderfully they are arranged, and what beautiful colours!"

"Yes, see the iridescent wings of this chap," and Uncle Jeff pointed to a fine specimen. "I don't wonder the old Egyptians loved this creature and carved their scarabs in its likeness, do you?"

"No, indeed," responded Dolly. "And do you like old Egyptian things, too? So do I. I saw wonders in the Museum."

"I have quite an antique collection, if you're interested."

"If I'm interested! Well, I just guess I *am!*"

The other girls enjoyed the exhibition, too, but not so much as Dolly, who was enthusiastic over it all. They had so far seen only the front rooms, but now Uncle Jeff conducted them to the room in the rear extension of the house, and as he unlocked the door he said, "Here are my greatest treasures of all."

The girls went in, and Mr. Forbes rolled up the shades and let in the sunlight.

"My, but it's close and stuffy!" exclaimed Bernice; "mayn't we have a window open, uncle?"

"Yes, indeed; I believe in fresh air, but I keep this room closed so much of the time it does get stale."

Mr. Forbes threw open a window that faced the

-〔156〕-

south, and as there was no wind blowing, the fresh winter air was balmy and pleasant.

"That's better," said Bernice, and she began to look at the treasures all about her.

There were many tall cases, like book-cases, and on their shelves were ranged curios and valuables of all sorts. These proved more interesting to Dotty than the birds and butterflies.

"Oh, look at the old jewellery!" she cried. "Just like what we saw in the museum, Doll."

"Yes, here are old Egyptian trinkets,— aren't they, Uncle Forbes?"

"Yes, those are Egyptian and Abyssinian. This nose ring was worn by a lady in India some centuries before you girls were born."

"What is the oldest thing you have, Uncle?" asked Alicia. "This jewellery?"

"No; this is my oldest piece," and Mr. Forbes took from a shelf an image of a cat. It was of dark brown material, and was dingy and roughened, as if by fire.

"This came from an old Egyptian tomb," he said. "You know they put all sorts of idols and charms in the tombs of their dead. Then once in a while these things are exhumed, and in some instances sold by the Egyptian Museum authorities. I buy only what is guaranteed by them to be genuine. I have an agent, who has travelled in many countries to collect authentic antiquities for me. This cat dates from about 2000 B. C."

"Gracious!" cried Dotty, "and there's been nearly two thousand years since B. C. That makes Mr. Cat about four thousand years old! Some cat!"

"Well, a cat has nine lives anyway," laughed Alicia, "so it ought to be a long time dead."

"That never was a live cat, was it?" asked Dolly.

"Oh, no. This was a bronze image, but fire and age have turned it to a mere brittle shell. If it were dropped to the floor it would break into a thousand pieces."

"Oh, my! take it!" exclaimed Dolly, who was holding the precious relic. "I didn't know it was so fragile."

Mr. Forbes took it carefully. "That's why I don't often bring young people up here. They're too heedless to appreciate the value of these old things. Yes, two centuries before the Christian Era, this piece of bric-a-brac, as we would call it, adorned the tomb of some Egyptian citizen. I have the guarantee, signed by the Egyptian Museum. And here is a fine specimen. This is in a better state of preservation. See, you can read the date on it clearly, 537 B. C."

Mr. Forbes took from a cabinet a small image of a mummy. It was of blue stone, somewhat chipped and worn, but preserving its shape and colour. On the back, in rude figures, but clearly discernible was the date to which he called their attention.

" Wonderful!" said Alicia. " Their figures are much like ours, aren't they? "

" Yes, my child, the Arabic numerals are of ancient usage. Think of the old hand that carved that date! Long since mouldered to dust!"

" It gives me the creeps!" declared Bernice, " and yet it fascinates me, too. Was this found in a tomb? "

" Yes, or in a temple. Excavations in Egypt, latterly, produce so many of these things that it is not difficult to get them. But that's pretty old, you see,— half a century before Christ."

"I wonder who was King of Egypt then," said Dotty. "I wish I could remember my history better. I learned about the Ptolemies and the other dynasties, but I get 'em all mixed up."

Although the others were eagerly examining the old mummy relic, Dolly stood looking at it thoughtfully.

"May I take it?" she said, after the others had scrutinised it.

Dolly handled it carefully, as she minutely observed it on every side. It was about six inches long and was a perfect little model of an Egyptian mummy. She gazed at the date deeply graven on the back, and then with a slight smile she handed it back to Mr. Forbes, saying, "Very good, Eddie!"

"What! What do you mean?" cried the old gentleman, glaring at her, and Alicia exclaimed, "Why, Dolly Fayre! You rude little thing!"

"But what do you mean?" persisted Mr. Forbes. "Why do you call me Eddie?"

"Oh," and Dolly laughed, "that's a slang phrase that people say when they see through a joke."

"Joke, miss! Are you making fun of my antiques? Explain yourself!"

"Yes, what *do* you mean, Dolly?" said Dotty, anxiously; "you can't mean to insult Mr. Forbes."

"You goosies!" cried Dolly, "he's fooling you. It's a joke on us."

"What is? What's a joke?"

"This mummy," and now Mr. Forbes had joined in Dolly's laughter.

"You're a cute one!" he said. "Not one person in a dozen catches on to that. Tell 'em, my dear. Oh, you *are* a smart one!"

Mr. Forbes shook with glee, and Dolly held up the image to the mystified girls.

"Don't you see, you blindies, the date 537 B. C. couldn't have been put on in the year 537 B. C.?"

"Why not?" asked Alicia, looking blank.

"Why, at that time they didn't know how many years it would be before Christ's birth. Nobody dated anything B. C. until after the Christian Era had begun."

"But why didn't they?" and Bernice also looked bewildered.

"Think a minute, you sillies. Nobody knew the exact date of the year one until after the year one was here. In fact, I don't think they began to count right away, anyhow. But certainly they didn't know five hundred and thirty-seven years before!"

"Oh, I see!" cried Bernice. "All the B. C. years have been computed or dated since the A. D. years began."

"Of course they have, and Mr. Forbes had the date carved on this mummy on purpose to fool people. Didn't you?"

"Yes," chuckled Mr. Forbes, "and it has fooled lots of people older and wiser than you, little Dolly Fayre! I think you're pretty smart to notice the fraud!"

"Oh, no. But it just happened to occur to me that I'd never seen a B. C. date marked before, and then I thought at once that it couldn't be."

"Pretty cute, all the same. You other girls didn't see it."

"No, we didn't," admitted Dotty. "I own up I was fooled. I never thought of the absurdity of the thing. Did you make up the joke?"

"No, I bought the mummy from a dealer who sold a few of them for the purpose of fun-making. It's a pretty good joke."

It was, and though the girls felt a little chagrined at being taken in, they were generous enough to appreciate Dolly's cleverness and be glad of it.

A case of antique jewellery proved interesting to all. The queer ornaments worn by the ancients were admired and studied by the girls, and Mr. Forbes enjoyed telling of their histories.

"This earring," he said, "is perhaps the gem of the whole collection. It is Byzantine, and is of wonderfully delicate workmanship."

The filigree gold ornament, was a long and slender pendant, of intricate gold work and studded with tiny jewels. It was one of a pair of earrings, and they wondered where its mate might be, if indeed, it was yet in existence.

"It would make a fine lavalliere," said Dolly, holding it up against her chest, and glancing in a nearby mirror. "See!" and she hooked the trinket into the lace at her throat, "isn't it becoming?"

"Very," laughed Bernice, and turned to see what Dotty was now exclaiming over.

It proved to be a bracelet, that legend said had been worn by Cleopatra, though Mr. Forbes frankly acknowledged he didn't believe this.

"Let me take it by the light," said Alicia, "it's getting dusk in here."

She took the bracelet to the open window, and admired the beauty of its wrought gold.

"Here, take it, Uncle Jeff," she said; "I declare I'm almost afraid to handle these valuable things for fear I should suddenly become a klep-what-do-you-call-it?"

"Kleptomaniac?" said her uncle, laughing. "I'm not afraid, or I shouldn't have brought you girls up here. I don't mind admitting I have one friend, a wise old octogenarian, rich as Crœsus, whom I wouldn't trust up here alone! He'd steal a gem as quickly as a highway robber would!"

"How awful!" said Bernice. "Just because of his craze for antiques?"

"Yes. You know some people are carried quite out of themselves by a pet hobby. Well, girls, it is getting dusk. Let's go downstairs, and have a little chat over what you've seen. I'd like to see how much you remember of what I've told you."

"Shall I shut the window, Uncle Jeff?" asked Bernice.

" No, leave it open. A little air will do the room good. I'll see to it later."

The girls left the room, Mr. Forbes followed, and locking the door, pocketed the key, and they all went downstairs.

CHAPTER XII

A PLEASANT hour was spent in the library, as Mr. Forbes told the girls anecdotes connected with his treasures, and also catechised them on what they had learned from their afternoon in his museum.

Dolly had taken the greatest interest in it, though Bernice soon proved that she had the best memory of them all, for she could tell dates and data that her uncle had informed them, and which the others more often forgot.

" I haven't any memory," sighed Dolly. " But I do love to see these things and hear about them. It's lots of work, isn't it, to get them all properly catalogued and labelled? "

" Yes, it keeps Fenn pretty busy, and often I bring in an assistant for him. But Fenn is a clever chap, and a quick worker."

Their chat was interrupted by Geordie Knapp and Ted Hosmer, who came over to call on the girls.

" Come right in, boys, glad to see you," was Mr. Forbes' hearty greeting. " I shouldn't wonder if our young friends here would be glad too. They've spent the whole afternoon with my old fogy talk and I'll warrant they'll be glad of a change."

" You stay with us, Uncle, and enjoy the change, too," laughed Alicia, as Mr. Forbes was leaving the room.

" No, no ; it doesn't seem to occur to you that *I*'d like a rest from a crowd of chatter-boxes!" His merry smile belied his words, and he went off leaving the young people together.

Mrs. Berry looked in, and hospitably invited the boys to stay to supper, which they willingly agreed to do.

Also, they stayed an hour or more after supper, and when at last they departed, the four girls remained in the library talking things over.

To their surprise, Mr. Forbes came to the room, and without a word sat down facing the group. Something in his expression caused the girls to stop their laughter and chatter, for the old gentleman looked decidedly serious.

" Well, my dears," and he looked from one to another, " have you had a pleasant day? "

" Yes, indeed," spoke up Alicia, and they all added words of assent.

" Well, I haven't," said Mr. Forbes, and they looked up at him with a startled air. " That is, I have just made a discovery that makes to-day one of the most unfortunate of my life."

" What is it, Uncle? What is the matter? " Alicia spoke solicitously, as if she feared her uncle had become suddenly ill.

" I have met with a loss."

" A loss? " queried Bernice. " What have you lost? "

" One of my dearest possessions. I went to my museum just now, to that rear room which we were in last, and I discovered that one of my valuable pieces of jewellery is gone."

The girls stared at him blankly, and at last, Bernice said, " Which one? "

" The Byzantine earring, the gold filigree piece."

" Oh," cried Alicia, " that lovely piece! Why, where can it be? "

" I don't know," replied her uncle, slowly. " I

searched everywhere, and as I couldn't find it, I came down here to ask if you girls had taken it as — as a joke on me."

"No, indeed!" exclaimed Alicia. "I'd scorn to do such a mean trick! None of us would think of such a thing, would we, girls?"

"No, indeed," said they all, and then a silence fell. Where could the jewel be? As always, in moments of excitement, Dolly turned very pale while Dotty flushed furiously red. Alicia, sat, her big eyes staring with dismay and Bernice nervously picked at her handkerchief.

"Come now," said Mr. Forbes, "if any of you girls did take it, in jest, give it up, for it isn't a funny joke at all."

"Oh, we didn't! I'm sure none of us did!" and Dolly almost wailed in her earnest denial.

"Of course, we didn't!" declared Dotty, angrily. "You ought to know we're not that sort of girls! It must have been mislaid, or pushed behind something that conceals it from view."

"Probably you're right," and Mr. Forbes looked at her intently. "That's probably the solution of its disappearance. I'll have Fenn make search to-morrow. I'm sorry I bothered you about it. Good-night."

With his funny abruptness he left the room, and the girls sat looking at each other in amazement.

"Did you ever hear anything like that!" demanded Dotty, furiously. "The idea of thinking we would do such a thing! I hate practical jokes, unless among a lot of school chums. I wouldn't think of playing a joke on a grown-up!"

"Uncle Jeff hasn't had much experience with young folks," put in Alicia, by way of excuse for their host. "You know he always lives alone, and he doesn't know what girls would or wouldn't do."

"But how awful for that thing to be lost," mused Bernice. "Suppose it fell down behind a case, or somewhere, and he *never* finds it!"

"Oh, his secretary will find it," said Dolly, hopefully. "It *must* be somewhere around. Don't let's talk about it. If we do, I shan't sleep a wink all night! I never do, if I worry."

"I think it's something to worry about," said Alicia. "It's the worst blow Uncle Jeff could have. You know how he adores his treasures. Why, he'd rather lose everything from these downstairs floors.

than one specimen out of those fourth story rooms. And that gold earring, of all things!"

"I tell you stop talking about it!" and Dolly clapped her hands over her ears. "Please, humour me in this," she added, smiling a little, "truly, it will keep me awake, if I get to worrying over it."

"All right, girls, let's drop the subject. Also, let's go to bed." It was Alicia who spoke, and she seemed under great excitement. Her eyes were un-naturally bright, and her cheeks were pink, and she moved jerkily, as if nervous.

So the four went up to their rooms, and saying good-night, they closed the door of communication between.

"What's the matter, Dollums?" asked Dotty, as she saw tears in the blue eyes.

"Nothing, Dot, only don't talk about that gold thing, will you? I just simply can't stand it if you do!"

"'Course I won't if you don't want me to, only what *do* you s'pose *did* become of it?"

"There you go! I think you're too mean for anything!"

"Oh, pshaw, I didn't mean to. I forgot. All

right, no more talk 'bout that old rubbish. What shall us talk about?"

"Don't talk at all. I'd rather go to sleep."

"Go, then, old crossy! But I s'pose you don't mean to sleep in your clothes!"

"No," and Dolly laughed a little. "I know I'm an old bear, and a crosspatch, and everything horrid,— but I'm nervous, Dotty, I *am*."

"I know it, old girl, but you'll get over it. I believe this city life is wearing you out! I believe it's time you went home."

"Oh, I think so, too. I wish we could go to-morrow!"

"Well, we can't. What has got into you, Dolly-rinda? I believe you're homesick!"

"I am, Dotty! I'd give anything to see mother now. I wish I was home in my own room."

"You'll be there soon enough. I s'pose we'll go Wednesday."

"Wednesday! that seems ages off!"

"Why, Dollums, to-morrow, you can say Wednesday is day after to-morrow! That's what I always do if I want to hurry up the days. But I don't want to hurry up our days in New York! No sir-ee! I love every one of 'em! *I* wish we **could** stay a month!"

"I don't!" and then there were few more words said between the two that night. Soon they were in bed, and if Dolly lay awake, Dotty didn't know it, for she fell asleep almost as soon as her dark curly head touched its pillow.

Meantime in the next room, the other two were talking.

"I do hope Uncle Jeff will find his old jewel," Bernice said, pettishly. "We won't have a bit more fun, if he doesn't."

"That's so," agreed Alicia, "but he won't find it."

"How do you know?"

"Oh, 'cause. It's very likely fallen down some crack or somewhere that nobody'd think of looking. Why, once, a photograph was on our mantel, and it disappeared most mysteriously. And we never could find it. And after years, there was a new mantel-piece put in, and there was the picture! It had slipped down a narrow mite of a crack between the mantel-shelf and the wall back of it."

"Tell Uncle Jeff that to-morrow. Maybe it will help him to find the thing."

" All right, I will. But of course, Mr. Fenn will look everywhere possible. I don't believe anybody'll ever find it."

" Then Uncle will be cast down and upset all the rest of the time we're here."

" Well, I can't help that. What do you suppose, Bernice, he asked us here for, anyway? "

" You ask me that a hundred dozen times a day, 'Licia! I tell you I don't know, but I think it was only a whim. You know how queer he is. He forgets we're in this house from one evening to the next. If to-day hadn't been Sunday, we wouldn't have seen him this afternoon. I wish we were going to stay another week."

" So do I. But I don't like to ask him outright, and he hasn't said anything about it lately. The others couldn't stay, anyway."

" Oh, I don't know. I think if they were invited their mothers would let them. And anyway, I'd rather stay without them, than to go home."

" Yes, I would, too. Dot likes it better than Dolly."

" Yes, Dolly's homesick. Anybody can see that. But they like it when we go to places, and see sights."

" Who wouldn't? We're really having fairy-tale times, you know."

" I know it. I shall hate to go back to school."

" Well, I don't hate to go home. I have good enough times in Berwick; but I'd like to stay here one week more. I think I'll ask Uncle Jeff to let us, if he doesn't ask us himself."

" Wait till he finds his lost treasure. He'll be pretty blue if he doesn't get that back."

" Yes, indeed he will. Let's hope the Fenn man will spy it out. It must be in that room somewhere, you know."

" Of course it must. The secretary will find it. That's what secretaries are for."

And then silence and sleep descended on that room also.

Next morning, Mr. Forbes appeared at the breakfast table. This was the first time they had ever seen him in the morning and the girls greeted him cheerily.

" Very nice," he said, affably, " to come down and breakfast with a flock of fresh young rosebuds like you," and he seemed so good-natured, that Alicia decided he had taken his loss more easily than she had feared.

But toward the end of the meal, Mr. Forbes made known the reason of his early appearance.

"We can't find that earring," he said, suddenly. "Mr. Fenn and I have been looking since six o'clock this morning. Now I'm going to ask you girls to help me. Will you all come up to the museum and hunt? Your young eyes may discern it, where we older seekers have failed. At any rate, I'd like you to try."

The four expressed ready willingness, and they rose from the table and followed Uncle Jeff up the stairs to the rear room where the loss had occurred.

The sun shone in at the southern windows, and flooded the room with brightness. It seemed impossible to overlook the treasure, and surely it must be found at once.

A youngish man was there before them, and he was introduced as the secretary. Lewis Fenn was a grave looking, solemn-faced chap, who, it was evident took seriously the responsibility of his position as tabulator and in part, custodian of valuable treasures. He bowed to the girls, but said nothing beyond a word of greeting to each.

"You see," said Mr. Forbes, "I locked this room myself, after you girls last evening, and nobody could get in to take the earring. Consequently, it would seem that a close search *must* be efficacious. So, let us all set to, and see what we can do in the way of discovery."

"Let's divide the room in four," suggested Mr. Fenn, "and one of you young ladies take each quarter."

"Good idea!" commented Uncle Jeff, "and we'll do just that. Alicia, you take this west end, next the door; Bernice, the east end, opposite; Dotty, the north side, and Dolly, the south side. There, that fixes it. Now, to work, all of you. I've exhausted my powers of search, and so has Fenn."

The two men sat down in the middle of the room, while the girls eagerly began to search. They were told not to look in the cases, but merely on tables or any place around the room where the jewel might have fallen or been laid.

"Who had it last?" asked Mr. Fenn, as the girls searched here and there.

Nobody seemed to know, exactly, and then Alicia said, suddenly, " Why, don't you know, Dolly hooked it onto the front of her dress, and said it would make a lovely pendant."

" But I took it off," said Dolly, turning white.

" Where did you put it then? " asked Mr. Fenn, not unkindly, but curiously.

" Let me see," faltered Dolly, " I don't quite remember. I guess I laid it on this table."

" If so, it must be there now, my dear," said Mr. Forbes, suavely. " Look thoroughly."

Dolly did look thoroughly, and Dotty came over to help her, but the earring was not on the table.

Nor was it on other tables that were about the room; nor on any chair or shelf or settee or window-sill.

" Where *can* it be? " said Dotty, greatly alarmed, lest Dolly's having fastened it to her dress should have been the means of losing it.

" Are you sure you removed it from your frock, Miss Fayre? " asked Fenn, and at that moment Dolly took a dislike to the man. His voice was low and pleasant, but the inflection was meaning, and he seemed to imply that Dolly might have worn it from the room.

"Of course, I am," Dolly replied, in a scared, low voice, which trembled as she spoke.

"There's an idea," said Mr. Forbes. "Mightn't you have left it hooked into your lace, Dolly, and it's there still? Run and look, my dear."

"I'll go with you," said Dotty, but Fenn said, "No, Miss Rose, you'd better stay here."

Dotty was so astonished at his dictum that she stood still and stared at him. Dolly ran off to her room on the second floor and carefully examined the dress she had worn the day before.

"No," she said, on her return, "it isn't on my dress. I knew it couldn't be,— I should have seen it when I undressed. Besides, I know I took it off here, only a moment after I tried it on. I merely looked at it an instant, and then I unhooked it and laid it on this table."

"But at first, you weren't sure that you did place it on that table, Miss Fayre," came the insinuating voice of Fenn once more.

"Yes, I did, I'm sure of it now," and Dolly's white face was drawn with anxiety.

"Think again," counselled the secretary. "Maybe you took it off, and absent-mindedly slipped it in your pocket."

CHAPTER XIII

SUSPICIONS

DOTTY turned on Fenn like a little fury.

"What do you mean?" she cried. "Are you accusing Dolly of stealing that thing?"

"There, there," said Mr. Forbes, placatingly. "Of course, Fenn didn't mean that. Not intentionally, that is. But without thinking, couldn't —"

"No, she couldn't!" stormed Dotty. "Dolly Fayre doesn't go around pocketing people's jewels unconsciously! She isn't a kleptomaniac, or whatever you call it! She did exactly as she says she did. She laid that earring on that table."

"Then why isn't it there now?" asked Fenn.

"Because somebody else moved it. Oh, don't ask me who. I don't *know* who! And I don't *care* who! But Dolly put it there, and whoever took it away from there can find it! Perhaps *you* can, Mr. Fenn!"

The secretary looked at the angry girl with an irritating smile.

"I wish I might, Miss Rose. But I've searched the room thoroughly, as you all have, too. It can't be *here*, you know."

"I'll tell you," said Alicia, eagerly, and then she described how in her home a photograph had slipped down behind the mantel and had been lost for years.

"Let us see," and Mr. Forbes went to the mantel in the room. But there was not the least mite of a crack between the shelf and the wall. Alicia's suggestion was useless.

"But," she said, "there might be that sort of a hiding-place somewhere else. Let's look all over."

The girls tried hard to find some crack or crevice in any piece of furniture, into which the trinket might have slipped, but there was none. They felt down between backs and seats of chairs, looked behind cases of treasures, moved every book and paper that lay on the tables, even turned up the edges of rugs, and peeped under.

"It doesn't make any difference how much we look," Dotty declared, "we've just got to look more, — that's all. Why, that earring is in this room, and that's all there is about that! Now, it's up to us to find it. You know, after you search all the possible places, you have to search the impossible ones."

"I admire your perseverance," said Mr. Forbes, "but I can't hope it will be rewarded. It isn't as if we were hunting for a thing that somebody had purposely concealed, that would mean an exhaustive search. But we're looking for something merely mislaid or tossed aside, and if we find it, it will be in some exposed place, not cleverly hidden."

"Oh, I don't know, Uncle Jeff," said Bernice, "you know when Alicia's photograph slipped behind the mantel, that was deeply hidden, although not purposely."

"Yes, that's so," and Uncle Jeff looked questioningly from one girl to another.

It was impossible to ignore the fact that he deemed one of them responsible for the disappearance of the jewel, and until the matter was cleared up, all felt under suspicion. Fenn, too, was studying the four young faces, as if to detect signs of guilt in one of them.

At last he said, "Let us get at this systematically. Who took the earring first, when Mr. Forbes handed it out from the case?"

"I did," said Dotty, promptly. "I stood nearest to Mr. Forbes and he handed it to me. After I looked at it, I passed it to Alicia."

"No, you didn't," contradicted Alicia. "I didn't touch it."

"Why, yes, 'Licia," Dotty persisted, "you took it and said —"

"I tell you I didn't! I never handled the things at all! It was Bernice."

"I did have it in my hands," said Bernice, reflectively, "but I can't remember whether I took it from Dot or Alicia."

"I didn't touch it, I tell you!" and Alicia frowned angrily.

"Oh, yes, you did," said Dolly, "it was you, Alicia, who passed it on to me. And I took it —"

"You didn't take it from me, Dolly," and Alicia grew red with passion. "I vow I never touched it! You took it from Bernice."

"No," said Dolly, trying to think. "I took it from you, and I held it up and asked you how it looked."

"No, Doll, you asked me that," said Bernice, "and I said it was very becoming."

"You girls seem decidedly mixed as to what you did," said Mr. Fenn, with a slight laugh. "I think you're not trying to remember very clearly."

"Hold on, Fenn," said Mr. Forbes, reprovingly. "It's in the girls' favour that they don't remember clearly. If they tossed the thing aside carelessly, they naturally wouldn't remember."

"But, Mr. Forbes," and the secretary spoke earnestly, "would these young ladies toss a valuable gem away carelessly? They are not ignorant children. They all knew that the earring is a choice possession. I'm sure not one of them would toss it aside, unheeding where it might fall!"

This was perfectly true. None of the four girls could have been so heedless as that! They had carefully handled every gem or curio shown them, and then returned it to Mr. Forbes as a matter of course.

Fenn's speech was rather a facer. All had to admit its truth, and the four girls looked from one to another and then at Mr. Forbes. He was studying them intently.

Bernice and Dolly were crying. Alicia and Dotty were dry-eyed and angry-faced. If one of the four had a secret sense of guilt, it was difficult to guess which one it might be, for all were in a state of excitement and were well-nigh hysterical.

"Much as I regret it," Mr. Forbes began, "I am forced to the conclusion that one or more of you girls knows something of the present whereabouts of my lost jewel. I do not say I suspect any of you of wilful wrong-doing, it might be you had accidentally carried it off, and now feel embarrassed about returning it. I can't — I won't believe, that any of you deliberately took it with intent to keep it."

"We thank you for that, Mr. Forbes," and Dotty's tone and the expression of her face denoted deepest sarcasm. "It is a comfort to know that you do not call us thieves! But, for my part, I think it is about as bad to accuse us of concealing knowledge of the matter. I think you'd better search our trunks and suitcases! And then, if you please, I should like to go home —"

"No doubt you would, Miss Rose!" broke in Fenn's cold voice. "A search of your belongings would be useless. If one of you is concealing the jewel, it would not be found in any available place of search. You would have put it some place in the house, not easy of discovery. That would not be difficult."

"Be quiet, Fenn," said Mr. Forbes. "Girls, I'm not prepared to say I think one of you has hidden the jewel, but I do think that some of you must know something about it. How can I think otherwise? Now, tell me if it is so. I will not scold,— I will not even blame you, if you have been tempted, or if having accidentally carried it off, you are ashamed to own up. I'm not a harsh man. I only want the truth. You can't be surprised at my conviction that you *do* know something of it. Why, here's the case in a nutshell. I handed that earring to you, and I never received it back. What can I think but that you have it yet? It is valuable, to be sure, but the money worth of it is as nothing to the awfulness of the feeling that we have an untrustworthy person among us. Can it be either of my two nieces who has done this wrong? Can it be either of their two young friends? I don't want to think so, but what alternative have I? And I *must* know! For reasons which I do not care to tell you, it is imperative that I shall discover who is at fault. I could let the whole matter drop, but there is a very strong cause why I should not do so. I beg of you, my dear nieces,— my dear young friends,— I beseech you, tell me the truth, won't you? "

Mr. Forbes spoke persuasively, and kindly.

Alicia burst into a storm of tears and sobbed wildly. Bernice, her face hidden in her handkerchief, was crying too.

Dotty sat stiffly erect in her chair, her little hands clenched, her big, black eyes staring at Mr. Forbes in a very concentration of wrath.

Dolly was limp and exhausted from weeping. With quivering lips and in a shaking voice, she said:

" Maybe one of us *is* a kleptomaniac, then, after all."

" Ah, a confession! " said Mr. Fenn, with his cynical little smile. " Go on, Miss Fayre. Which one has the accumulating tendency? "

" You do make me so mad! " exclaimed Dotty, glaring at him. " Uncle Forbes, can't we talk with you alone? "

" Oh, no, little miss," said Fenn, " Mr. Forbes is far too easy-going to look after this affair by himself! He'd swallow all the stories you girls would tell him! I'll remain, if you please. Unless you have something to conceal, you can't object to my presence at this interesting confab."

Dolly came to Dotty's aid. She looked at the secretary with a glance of supreme contempt.

"It is of no consequence, Mr. Fenn," she said, haughtily, "whether you are present or not. Uncle Forbes, I agree with Dotty. You said yourself, you have an acquaintance who can't help taking treasures that are not his own. It may be that one of us has done this. But, even so, the jewel must be in the house. None of us has been out of the house since we were in this room yesterday afternoon. So, if it is in the house, it must be found."

"Ha! You *have* hidden it securely, to be willing to have a thorough search of the house made!" and Fenn looked unpleasantly at her. "Own up, Miss Fayre; it will save a lot of trouble for the rest of us."

Dolly tried to look at the man with scorn, but her nerves gave way, and again she broke down and cried softly, but with great, convulsive sobs.

Dotty was furious but she said nothing to Fenn for she knew she would only get the worst of it.

"Come now, Dolly," said Mr. Forbes, in a gentle way, "stop crying, my dear, and let's talk this over. Where did you lay the earring when you took it from your dress?"

"On — on — the t-table," stammered Dolly, trying to stop crying. But, as every one knows, it is not an easy thing to stem a flood of tears, and Dolly couldn't speak clearly.

"Yes; what table?"

"This one," and Dotty spoke for her, and indicated the table by the south window.

"Where,— on the table?" persisted Uncle Jeff. Dolly got up and walked over to the light stand in question.

"About here, I think," and she indicated a spot on the surface of the dull finished wood.

"Why didn't you hand it back to me?" queried Mr. Forbes, in a kind tone.

"I d-don't know, sir," Dolly sobbed again. "I'm sure I don't know why I didn't."

"I know," put in Dotty. "Because just then, Mr. Forbes showed us a bracelet that had belonged to Cleopatra, and we all crowded round to look at that, and Doll laid down the earring to take up the bracelet. We didn't suppose we were going to be accused of stealing!"

"Tut, tut," said Mr. Forbes. "Nobody has used that word! I don't accuse you of anything,— except carelessness."

"But when it comes to valuable antiques," interrupted Fenn, "it is what is called criminal carelessness."

"It *was* careless of Dolly to lay the earring down," said Mr. Forbes, "but that is not the real point. After she laid it down, just where she showed us, on that small table, somebody must have picked it up. Her carelessness in laying it there might have resulted in its being brushed off on the floor, but not in its utter disappearance."

"Maybe it fell out of the window," suggested Bernice, suddenly, "that window was open then, you know."

Mr. Forbes walked over to the table. "No," he said, "this stand is fully a foot from the window sill. It couldn't have been unknowingly brushed as far as that."

"Of course, it couldn't," said Fenn, impatiently. "You're making no progress at all, Mr. Forbes."

"Propose some plan, yourself, then," said Dotty, shortly; "you're so smart, suppose you point your finger to the thief!"

"I hope to do so, Miss Rose," and Fenn smirked in a most aggravating way. "But I hesitate to accuse anyone before I am quite sure."

"A wise hesitation!" retorted Dotty. "Stick to that, Mr. Fenn!"

She turned her back on him, and putting her arm round Dolly, sat in silent sympathy.

Suddenly Bernice spoke. She was not crying now, on the contrary, she was composed and quiet.

"Uncle Jeff," she said, "this is a horrid thing that has happened. I feel awfully sorry about it all, but especially because it is making so much trouble for Dolly and Dotty, the two friends that I brought here. Alicia and I belong here, in a way, but the others are our guests, as well as your guests. It is up to us, to free them from all suspicion in this thing and that can only be done by finding the earring. I don't believe for one minute that any one of us four girls had a hand, knowingly, in its disappearance, but if one of us did, she must be shown up. I believe in fairness all round, and while I'm sure the jewel slipped into some place, or under or behind something, yet if it *didn't*,— if somebody did, — well,— steal it! we must find out who. I wouldn't be willing, even if you were, Uncle, to let the matter drop. I want to know the solution of the mystery, and I'm going to find it!"

"Bravo! Bernie, girl," cried her uncle, "that's the talk! As I told you I must know the truth of this thing,— never mind why, I *must* find it out. But how?"

"First," said Bernice, speaking very decidedly, but not looking toward the other girls, "I think all our things ought to be searched."

"Oh, pshaw, Bernie," said Alicia, "that would be silly! You know if any of us wanted to hide that earring we wouldn't put it in among our clothes."

"Why not?" demanded Bernice. "I can't imagine any of us having it, but if we have, it's by accident. Why, it might have caught in any of our dresses or sashes, and be tucked away there yet."

"That's so," and Dotty looked hopeful. "It could be, that as one of us passed by the table, it got caught in our clothing. Anyway, we'll all look."

"But don't look in your own boxes," objected

Fenn. "Every girl must search another's belongings."

"I wonder you'd trust us to do *that!*" snapped Dotty, and Fenn immediately replied:

"You're right! It wouldn't be safe! I propose that Mrs. Berry search all your rooms."

"Look here, Fenn, you are unduly suspicious," Mr. Forbes remonstrated, mildly.

"But, sir, do you want to get back your gem, or not? You asked for my advice and help in this matter, now I must beg to be allowed to carry out my plans of procedure."

It was plain to be seen that Mr. Forbes was under the thumb of his secretary. And this was true. Lewis Fenn had held his position for a long time, and his services were invaluable to Jefferson Forbes. It was necessary that the collector should have a reliable, responsible and capable man to attend to the duties he required of a secretary, and these attributes Fenn fully possessed. But he was of a small, suspicious nature, and having decided on what course to pursue regarding the lost curio, he was not to be swerved from his path.

"Well, well, we will see," Mr. Forbes said, an

anxious look wrinkling his forehead as he looked at the girls. "Run away now, it's nearly luncheon time. Don't worry over the thing. Each one of you knows her own heart. If you are innocent, you've no call to worry. If you are implicated, even in a small degree in the loss of my property, come to me and tell me so. See me alone, if you like. I will hear your confession, and if it seems wise, I will keep it confidential. I can't promise this, for as I hinted, I have a very strong reason for probing this affair to the very core. It is a mystery that *must* be cleared up!"

CHAPTER XIV

AT THE TEA ROOM

THE girls went to their rooms to tidy up for luncheon, though there was some time before the meal would be announced.

By common consent the door was closed between the rooms, and on one side of it the two D's faced each other.

"Did you ever see such a perfectly horrid, hateful, contemptible old thing as that Fenn person?" exclaimed Dotty, her voice fairly shaken with wrath. "I can't see how Mr. Forbes can bear to have him around! He ought to be excommunicated, or whatever they do to terrible people!"

"He *is* awful, Dotty, I don't wonder you gave it to him! But you mustn't do it. He's Mr. Forbes' right hand man, and whatever Uncle Jeff tells him to do, he'll do it. The idea of searching our trunks! I won't allow them to touch mine, I can tell you that!"

"Oh, Dolly, now don't be stubborn. Why, for you to refuse to let them look over your things would be the same as saying you had the thing hidden."

"Dorothy Rose! What a thing to say to me!"

"I'm not saying it to you! I mean, I am saying it to you, just to show you what other people would say! You know it, Dolly. You know Fenn would say you had the earring."

"But, Dotty, it must be somewhere."

"Of course, it must be somewhere,— look here, Dollyrinda, you don't know anything about it, do you? Honest Injun?"

"How you talk, Dot. How should I know anything about it?"

"But do you?"

"Don't be silly."

"But, *do* you?"

"Dotty, I'll get mad at you, if you just sit there saying, 'But do you?' like a talking machine! Are you going to change your dress for luncheon?"

"No, I'm not. These frocks are good enough. But, Dolly, *do* you? do you know anything, *anything* at all, about the earring?"

Dolly was sitting on the edge of her little white

bed. At Dotty's reiteration of her query, Dolly threw her head down on the pillow and hid her face.

" Do you? " repeated Dotty, her voice now tinged with fear.

Dolly sat upright and looked at her. " Don't ask me, Dotty," she said, " I can't tell you."

" Can't tell me," cried Dotty, in bewilderment, " then who on earth *could* you tell, I'd like to know! "

" I could tell mother! Oh, Dotty, I want to go home! "

" Well, you can't go home, not till day after to-morrow, anyway. What's the matter with you, Dolly, why can't you tell me what you know? How can I find the thing, and clear you from suspicion if you have secrets from me? "

" You can't, Dotty. Don't try."

Dolly spoke in a tense, strained way, as if trying to preserve her calm. She sat down at their little dressing-table and began to brush her hair.

A tap came at the door, and in a moment, Bernice came in.

" Let me come in and talk to you girls," she

begged. "Alicia is in a temper, and won't say anything except to snap out something quarrelsome. What are we going to do?"

"I don't know, Bernie," and Dotty looked as if at her wits' end. "It's bad enough to put up with that old Fenn's hateful talk, but now Dolly's gone queer, and you say Alicia has,— what *are* we to do?"

"Let's talk it all over with Mrs. Berry at lunch, she's real sensible and she's very kind-hearted."

"Yes, she is. And there's the gong now. Come on, let's go down. Come on, Dollikins, brace up, and look pretty! Heigho! come on, Alicia!"

Alicia appeared, looking sullen rather than sad, and the quartette went downstairs.

Mrs. Berry listened with interest to their story. Interest that quickly turned to deep concern as the story went on.

"I don't like it," she said, as the girls paused to hear her comments. "No carelessness or thoughtlessness could make that valuable earring disappear off the face of the earth! I mean, it couldn't get *lost*, it must have been taken."

"By us?" flared out Alicia.

"Maybe not meaningly, maybe for a joke, maybe
-⟨199⟩-

unconsciously; but it was carried out of that room by some one, of that I'm certain."

"The idea of thinking we'd do it as a joke!" cried Bernice.

"But you told me about the joke Mr. Forbes played on you about the B. C. image, why mightn't one of you have taken this to tease him? Oh, girls, if any of you did,— give it back, I beg of you! Mr. Forbes is a kind man, but a very just one. If you give it back at once, and explain, he will forgive you, fully and freely. But if you delay too long he will lose patience. And, too, you must know he wants to —"

"Wants to what, Mrs. Berry?" asked Dotty, for the lady had stopped speaking very suddenly.

"Never mind. I forgot myself. But Mr. Forbes has a very strong reason for wishing to sift this matter to the bottom. Don't, girls,— oh, *don't* deceive him!"

"What makes you think we're deceiving him?" cried Dotty. "That's the way old Fenn talks! Isn't he a disagreeable man, Mrs. Berry?"

"Mr. Fenn is peculiar," she admitted, "but it

isn't nice for you to criticise Mr. Forbes' secretary. He is a trusted employé, and of great use in his various capacities."

" But he was very rude to us," complained Alicia. " He was positively insulting to Dolly and me."

" Don't remember it," counselled Mrs. Berry. " The least you have to do with him the better. Forget anything he may have said, and keep out of his way all you can."

Mr. Forbes' housekeeper was a tactful and peaceable woman, and she well knew the temperament and disposition of the secretary. She herself disliked him exceedingly, but it was part of her diplomacy to avoid open encounter with him. And she deemed it best for the girls to follow her course.

" I think," she said finally, " the best thing for you to do, is to go for a nice motor ride in the park. It is a lovely day, and the ride will do you good and make you feel a heap better. Then on your return, stop at a pretty tearoom, and have some cakes and chocolate, or ices; and while you're gone, I'll have a little talk with Mr. Forbes, and, who knows, maybe we might find the earring!"

"You're going to search our boxes!" cried Alicia. "Well, I won't submit to such an insult! I shall lock mine before I go out."

"So shall I," declared Dolly. "I think we all ought to. Really, Mrs. Berry, it's awful for you to do a thing like that!"

"Mercy me! girls, how you do jump at conclusions! I never said a word about searching your rooms. I had no thought of such a thing! You mustn't condemn me unheard! You wouldn't like that, yourselves!"

"Indeed, we wouldn't, Mrs. Berry," cried Dolly, smiling at her. "I apologise for my burst of temper, I'm sure. But I hate to be suspected."

"Be careful, Dolly, not to be selfish. Others hate to be suspected too —"

"Yes, but *I'm* innocent!" cried Dolly, and as soon as she had spoken she blushed fiery red, and her sweet face was covered with confusion.

"Meaning somebody else *isn't* innocent!" spoke up Alicia; "who, please?"

"Me, probably," said Dotty, striving to turn the matter off with a laugh. "Dolly and I always suspect each other on principle —"

"Oh, pooh! This is no time to be funny!" and Alicia looked daggers at the smiling Dotty.

"You're right, Alicia, it isn't!" she flashed back, and then Mrs. Berry's calm voice interrupted again.

"Now, girlies, don't quarrel among yourselves. There's trouble enough afoot, without your adding to it. Take my advice. Go and put on some pretty dresses and then go for a ride, as I told you, and get your tea at the 'Queen Titania' tearoom. It's just lately been opened, and it's a most attractive place. But promise not to squabble. Indeed, I wish you'd promise not to discuss this matter of the earring. But I suppose that's too much to ask!"

"Yes, indeed, Mrs. Berry," and Bernice smiled at her. "I'm sure we couldn't keep that promise if we made it!"

"Well, don't quarrel. It can't do any good. Run along now, and dress."

The cheery good-nature of the housekeeper helped to raise the girls' depressed spirits, and after they had changed into pretty afternoon costumes and donned their coats and furs, they had at least, partially forgotten their troubles of the morning.

But not for long. As they sped along in the

great, comfortable car, each found her thoughts re-
verting to the sad episode, and oh, with what varied
feelings!

Suddenly, Bernice broke out with a new theory.

"I'll tell you what!" she exclaimed; "Uncle Jet.
hid that thing himself, to see how we would act!
Then he pretended to suspect us! That man is
studying us! Oh, you needn't tell *me!* I've noticed
it ever since we came. He watches everything we
do, and when he says anything especial, he looks
closely, to see how we're going to take it."

"I've noticed that, too," agreed Dolly. "But
it's silly, Bernie, to think he took his own jewel."

"Just to test us, you know. I can't make out
why he wants to study us so, but maybe he's writing a book or something like that. Else why did he
want not only Alicia and me but two of our friends
to come for this visit? He studies us, not only as
to our own characters, but the effect we have on
each other."

Dotty looked at Bernice with interest.

"You clever thing!" she cried; "I do believe
you're right! I've caught Uncle Forbes frequently
looking at one or another of us with the most quiz-

zical expression and listening intently for our answers to some question of right or wrong or our opinions about something."

"I've noticed it," said Dolly, though in an indifferent tone, "but I don't think he's studying us. I think he's so unused to young people that everything we do seems strange to him. Why any of our fathers would know what we're going to say before we say it. Mine would anyhow and so would Dot's. But Mr. Forbes is surprised at anything we say or do because he never saw girls at close range before. I think we interest him just like his specimens do."

"That's it," cried Dotty, "you've struck it, Doll. We're just specimens to him. He's studying a new kind of creature! And, maybe he did want to see what we'd do in given circumstances,— like an unjust accusation, and so he arranged this tragic situation."

"No," said Dolly, still in that unnerved, listless way, "no, that won't do, Dotty. If it were true, he'd never let Mr. Fenn be so rude to us. Why, this morning, I'm sure,— I *know*,— Mr. Forbes was just as uncertain of what had become of that earring as — as any of us were."

"Well, have it your own way," and Dotty smiled good-naturedly at her chum, "but here's my decision. That thing is lost. Somehow or other, for some ridiculous reason, blame seems to be attached to my Dollyrinda. I won't stand it! I hereby announce that I'm going to find that missing gimcrack before I go back to my native heath,— if I have to take all summer!"

"Aren't you going home on Wednesday?" cried Dolly, looking aghast at the idea.

"Not unless that old thing is found! I'll telephone my dear parents not to look for me until they see me. I'll hunt every nook and cranny of Mr. Forbes' house, and when I get through, I'll hunt over again. But find the thing, I will! So there, now!"

"Why do you say Dolly is suspected?" asked Alicia.

"Oh, you all know she is, just because she hooked the foolish thing into her lace. She put it on the table after that, and every one of us probably handled it, but no, it is laid to Dolly! Just because she's the only one of us incapable of such a thing, — I guess!"

"Why, Dot Rose, what a speech!" and Dolly al-

-《206》-

most laughed at the belligerent Dotty. "None of us would take it wrongly, I'm sure — but —"

"Well, but what?" demanded Alicia, as Dolly paused.

"Oh, nothing, Alicia, but the same old arguments. Mistake,— unintentional,— caught in our dresses, — and all that." Dolly spoke wearily, as if worn out with the subject.

"Well, I've a new theory," said Dotty, "I believe that Fenn man stole it!"

The other three laughed, but Dotty went on, "Yes, I do. You see, he's never had a chance to take any of the treasures before, 'cause Uncle Forbes would know he was the thief. But now he has all us four to lay it on, so he made the most of his chance."

"Oh, Dotty, I can't believe it!" said Bernice. "He didn't act like a thief this morning. He was more like an avenging justice."

"That's just his smartness! Make it seem as if we did it, you know."

"Nothing in it," and Dolly smiled at Dotty's theory. "He wasn't here yesterday, at all. He didn't know that I hooked the old thing on my waist, — oh, I *wish* I hadn't done that!"

"Never you mind, Dollums," Dotty said, endear-ingly. "If he did do it, we'll track him down. Be-cause, girls, I tell you I'm going to find that earring. And what Dorothy Rose says, goes! See?"

Dotty's brightness cheered up the others, and as they drove through the park, there were many sights of interest, and after a time the talk drifted from the subject that had so engrossed them.

And when at last they stopped at the new tea room and went in, the beauty and gaiety of the place made them almost forget their trouble.

"I'll have *café parfait*," said Dotty, "with heaps of little fancy cakes. We can't get real *fancy* cakes in Berwick, and I do love 'em!"

The others were of a like mind, and soon they were feasting on the rich and delicate confections that the modern tea room delights to provide.

While they sat there, Muriel Brown came in, ac-companied by two of her girl friends.

"Oh, mayn't we chum with you?" Muriel cried, and our four girls said yes, delightedly.

"How strange we should meet," said Dolly, but Muriel laughed and responded, "Not so very, as I'm here about four or five days out of the seven. I just simply love the waffles here, don't you? "

And then the girls all laughed and chattered and the New Yorkers invited the other four to several parties and small affairs.

" New York is the most hospitable place I ever saw! " declared Dotty. " We seem to be asked somewhere every day for a week."

" Everybody's that," laughed Muriel. " But you must come to these things we're asking you for, won't you? "

" I don't believe we can promise," said Bernice, suddenly growing serious. " You see, we may go home on Wednesday."

" Day after to-morrow? Oh, impossible! Don't say the word! " And with a laugh, Muriel dashed away the unwelcome thought. " I shall depend upon you," she went on, " especially for the Friday party. That's one of the best of all! You just *must* be at it! "

" If we're here, we will," declared Alicia, carried away by the gay insistence. " And I'm 'most sure Bernice and I will be here, even if the others aren't."

"I want you all," laughed Muriel, "but I'll take as many as I can get."

Then into the limousine again, and off for home.

"Oh," cried Dolly, "that horrid business! I had almost forgotten it!"

"We can't forget it till it's settled," said Dotty, and her lips came tightly together with a grim expression that she showed only when desperately in earnest.

CHAPTER XV

DOLLY'S RIDE

IT was Tuesday morning that Lewis Fenn came to Dolly and asked her to give him a few moments' chat.

A little bewildered, Dolly followed Fenn into the reception room, and they sat down, Fenn closing the door after them.

"It's this way, Miss Fayre," he began. "I know you took the gold earring. It's useless for you to deny it. It speaks for itself. You are the only one of you girls especially interested in antiques, and moreover, you are the one who handled the jewel last. Now, I don't for a moment hold you guilty of stealing. I know that you thought the thing of no very great intrinsic value, and as Mr. Forbes has so many such things in his possession you thought one more or less couldn't matter to him. So, overcome by your desire to keep it as a souvenir, and because of its antique interest you involuntarily took it away

with you. Of course, searching your boxes is useless, for you have concealed it some place in the
house where no one would think of looking. Now, I
come to you as a friend, and advise you to own up.
I assure you, Mr. Forbes will forgive you and he will
do so much more readily if you go to him at once and
confess."

Dolly sat rigidly, through this long citation, her
face growing whiter, her eyes more and more frightened, as she listened. When Fenn paused, she strug-
gled to speak but couldn't utter a sound. She was
speechless with mingled emotions. She was angry,
primarily, but other thoughts rushed through her
brain and she hesitated what attitude to assume.

The secretary looked at her curiously.

" Well? " he said, and there was a threatening tone
in his voice.

Dolly looked at him, looked straight into his accusing eyes, began to speak, and then, in a burst of
tears, she cried out, " Oh, how I *hate* you!"

Dotty flung open the door and walked in.

" I've been listening," she announced, " listening at
the keyhole, to hear what you said to my friend! I
heard, and I will answer you. Dolly Fayre no more

took that earring, than you did, Mr. Fenn, and I'm inclined to think from your manner, that you stole it yourself ! "

" What ! " shouted Fenn, surprised out of his usual calm. " What do you mean, you little minx ? "

" Just what I say," repeated Dotty, but Dolly had already fled from the room. She went in search of Mrs. Berry, and found her in her own bedroom.

" Please, Mrs. Berry," said Dolly, controlling her sob-shaken voice, " I want to go out, all by myself, a little while. May I ? "

" Goodness, child, what do you mean? Where? I'll go with you."

" No; I want to go alone. I have to think something out all by myself. Nobody can help me, and if I'm here, all the girls will butt in and bother me."

" Where are you going? For a walk ? "

" No, please. I want to ride on the top of a Fifth Avenue stage. I want to go alone, and then, sitting up there, with the fresh air blowing around me, I can think something out. I may go, mayn't I, Mrs. Berry? I know all about the stages."

" Why, yes, child, of course, you can go, if you really want to. You can't come to any harm just riding on top of a bus. Run along. But I'd rather you'd let me help you. Or go with you."

" No, please; I must be alone. I don't want even Dotty. I have something very serious to decide. No one can help me. My mother could, but she isn't here."

" I wish you'd try me," and the kind lady smiled endearingly.

" I would if I could, and you're a dear to ask me. But this is a special matter, and it troubles me awfully. So, I'll go off by myself for an hour or so, and when I come back, I'll be all decided about it."

Dolly got her hat and coat, without seeing the other girls at all. She went out at the front door of the big Fifth Avenue house, and walked a few blocks before she stopped to wait for a stage.

" I don't care which way I go," she thought to herself, " I'll take the first bus that comes along."

The first one chanced to be going down-town, and signalling the conductor, Dolly climbed the little winding stairs to the top.

There were only half a dozen passengers up there, and Dolly sat down near the front.

It was a clear, crisp morning. The air was full of

ozone, and no sooner had Dolly settled herself into
her seat, than she began to feel better. Her mind
cleared and she could combat the problems that were
troubling her. But she was in a dilemma. Should
she go to Mr. Forbes and tell him where the jewel
was,— or, should she not?

She wanted to be honest, she wanted to do right,
but it would be a hard task. The more she thought
it over, the more she was perplexed, and though her
spirits were cheered by the pleasant ride, her troubles
were as far as ever from a solution.

Down she went, down the beautiful Avenue, past
the Sherman statue and the Plaza fountain. On,
past the Library, down through the shopping dis-
trict, and then Dolly concluded she would go on down
to the Washington Arch, and stay in the same bus
for the return trip.

But, before she realised it, she found the bus she
was in had turned East on Thirty-second Street, and
was headed for the Railroad Station. She started
up, to get off the stage, but sat down again.

"What's the use?" she thought. "I can just as
well go on to the station, and come back again. I
only want the ride."

So she went on, and at the station, she was asked to take another stage. Down the stairs she climbed, and as she glanced at the great colonnade of the building she realised that from there trains went home! Home,— where mother was!

Unable to resist, Dolly obeyed an impulse to enter the station.

The warm, pleasant atmosphere of the arcade, soothed her nerves, and she walked along, thinking deeply.

She came to the stairs that led down to the waiting rooms, and a great wave of homesickness came over her.

She would go home! She had money with her, she would buy a ticket, and go straight to Berwick! She couldn't, she simply *could not* face Uncle Jeff and the girls, with her secret untold, and she would not tell it!

Anyway, she couldn't go back to the house where that horrid Fenn was! That was certain.

She looked in her pocket-book, and tucked away in its folds was the return half of her Berwick ticket. She had forgotten that she had it with her. It seemed a finger of Fate pointing the way.

" I will," she decided. " I will go back to Berwick. I'll ask about the trains."

Inquiry at the Information Department told her that there would be a train for Berwick in half an hour, and Dolly went in and sat down in the waiting room.

Suddenly it struck her that the people at Mr. Forbes' would be alarmed at her non-appearance, and would be very anxious for her safety.

That would never do. She had no wish to disturb kind Mrs. Berry or to scare Dotty half to death.

She saw the telephone booths near by, and realised how easy it would be to communicate with the house.

She asked the operator for the number of Jefferson Forbes' residence and in a moment was in the booth.

The butler responded to her call, and Dolly did not ask for any one else.

" That you, McPherson? " she said, speaking as casually as she could.

" Yes, Miss Fayre. Will you speak with Mrs. Berry? "

" No; I'll give you a message. Please say to Miss Rose that I have gone to Berwick."

" To Berwick, miss? "

" Yes; and tell Mrs. Berry the same. That's all, McPherson; no message for any one else."

" Yes, Miss Fayre. When will you be back, Miss Fayre? "

" Not at all. Or, that is,— never mind that. Just say I have gone to Berwick. I'll write to Miss Rose as soon as I get there."

" Yes, Miss Fayre," and the butler hung up his receiver. It was not his business if the ladies came or went.

In obedience to orders, McPherson went to Mrs. Berry and delivered the message.

" The dear child," said the housekeeper, and the tears came to her eyes. Of course, she knew about the earring episode, and until now she hadn't suspected that Dolly really took it. But to run away practically proved her guilt. So she had meant to go when she asked permission to go on the bus! Mrs. Berry's heart was torn, for she loved Dolly best of the four, and it was a blow to be thus forced to believe her guilty. She quizzed the butler, but he had no further information to give.

" She only said she was going, ma'am, and said for me to tell you and Miss Rose. That's all."

"I will tell Miss Rose," said Mrs. Berry, and dismissed the man.

She thought deeply before going to find Dotty. She wondered if she might yet stay Dolly's flight and persuade her to return. She looked up a timetable, and found that the train for Berwick would leave in ten minutes. Doubtless Dolly was already in the car.

However, being a woman of energetic nature, Mrs. Berry telephoned to the Railroad Station. She asked for a porter, and begged him to try to find Dolly, whom she described, and ask her to come to the telephone.

"I remember seeing that girl," said the negro porter. "She was walking around sort of sadlike, and sort of uncertain. But I don't see her now."

"Look on the Berwick train," commanded Mrs. Berry, "and do it quickly. If she's on the train, ask her to get off and answer my call. I think she'll do it. Go quickly! I'll hold the wire."

But it was within a few minutes of starting time; the train was crowded, and after a short search the porter came back with the word that he couldn't find her. " I could of," he said, " if I'd 'a' had a minute more. But the Train Despatcher put me off, and they started. Sorry, ma'am."

" I'm sorry, too," and Mrs. Berry sighed as she realised how near she had come to success, only to fail.

She thought a few moments longer, then she went to find Dotty.

That young person, she discovered, to her astonishment, was up in Mr. Forbes' own study, on the fourth floor. Dotty had insisted on an interview with her host after the stormy time she had with his secretary.

Mr. Forbes had received her, not at all unwillingly, for he wanted to get at the truth of the unpleasant matter.

" Dolly never took it ! " Mrs. Berry heard Dotty declare, as she approached the door. " Either it's just lost, or else Mr. Fenn stole it,— or else —"

" Or else what? " asked Mr. Forbes, as Dotty paused.

" I don't like to say," and Dotty twisted her finger nervously ; " I do suspect somebody,— at least, I fear maybe I do, a little bit, but I won't say anything about it, unless you keep on blaming Dolly. Then I will!"

"I have something to tell you," said Mrs. Berry, entering. "Dolly has gone home."

"What!" cried Mr. Forbes and Dotty simultaneously. Lewis Fenn smiled.

"Yes," continued Mrs. Berry, "she has gone home to Berwick. She came to me and asked if she might go for a ride on top of a Fifth Avenue stage, to think things out by herself,— she said. Then, a little later, she telephoned from the Pennsylvania Station that she was just taking the train for Berwick."

"I don't believe it!" cried Dotty. "Who told you?"

"McPherson. He took the message. Dolly said to tell you, Dotty, and to tell me, but she sent no word to any one else."

"Looks bad," said Mr. Forbes, shaking his head.

"I told you so!" said Lewis Fenn, nodding his. "I knew when I flatly accused Miss Fayre this morning of taking the earring, that she was the guilty one. Understand me, she didn't mean to steal. She didn't look upon it as theft. She only took a fancy to the bauble, and appropriated it without really thinking it wrong. As a child would take a worthless little trinket, you know."

Dotty looked stunned. She paid no attention to Fenn's talk; she stared at Mrs. Berry, saying, " Has she really gone? "

" Yes, dear," answered the sympathetic lady, " she has. Perhaps it's the best thing. She'll tell her mother all about it, and then we'll know the truth."

" Yes, she'll confess to her mother," said Fenn, and he grinned in satisfaction.

" Shut up, Fenn," said Mr. Forbes. " I'm not at all sure Dolly is the culprit. If I know that girl, she wouldn't run away if she were guilty,— but she might if she were unjustly accused."

" That's generous of you, sir," said the secretary, " but you know yourself that when I taxed Miss Fayre definitely with the deed, she immediately went off, pretending that she was just going for a ride, and would return. That piece of deception doesn't look like innocence, I think you must admit ! "

" No, no, it doesn't. Dotty, did you say you had some other suspicion? What is it? "

" I can't tell it now. I can't understand Dolly. I know, oh, I *know* she never took the earring, but I can't understand her going off like that. She never pretends. She's never deceitful —"

" She surely was this time," and Fenn seemed to exult in the fact.

" Maybe she changed her plan after she started," suggested Dotty delorously.

" Not likely," mused Mr. Forbes. " It was unprecedented for her to go alone for a bus ride, but if it was because she wanted to get off home secretly, it is, of course, very plausible. She didn't want any of you girls to know she was going, lest you persuade her not to. She didn't want to go in my car alone, as that would seem strange. But to take a bus, that was really a clever way to escape unnoticed!"

" I'm surprised that she telephoned back at all," said Mr. Fenn.

" Of course, she would!" said Dotty, indignantly. " She didn't want us to think she was lost or worry about her safety."

" She was most considerate," said Fenn, sarcastically.

" Oh, stop!" cried Dotty, at the very end of her patience with the man. " You're enough to drive any one distracted!"

"Let the child alone, Fenn," said Mr. Forbes; "your manner *is* irritating."

"The whole affair is irritating," returned the secretary, "but it is now in a way to be cleared up, I think. We shall hear from Miss Fayre's parents, I'm sure."

"What *is* going on?" spoke up Alicia from the doorway, and she and Bernice came into the room. "I know we're forbidden up here, but Dotty's here, so we came, too. What's the matter?"

"Dolly's gone home," said Mr. Forbes, looking at his nieces.

"Dolly has!" exclaimed Bernice. "What for?"

"Because she was persecuted!" Dotty replied, "and unjustly accused, and suspected, and her life made generally miserable! I don't blame her for going home! I'm going, too."

"When did she go? Who took her?" Alicia asked.

"She went alone," said Mrs. Berry, and she gave them the details of Dolly's departure.

"Well, I am surprised," said Bernice, but Alicia began to cry softly.

"Yes, cry, Alicia!" said Dotty, turning on her.

" I should think you *would!* *You* made Dolly go!
You know where that earring thing is ! "

" I do not ! " and Alicia stared at Dotty.

" Well, you know something more than you've
told ! "

CHAPTER XVI

WAS IT ALICIA?

"WHAT do you mean by that speech, Dotty?" asked Bernice, as Alicia kept on crying.

"I mean just what I say. Alicia knows where the earring is, or, if she doesn't know that, she knows something about it that she won't tell us."

"What is it, Alicia?" said her uncle, kindly. "If you know anything at all, tell us, won't you?"

"I don't, Uncle. I don't know *anything* about it!" and Alicia wept more than ever.

"Well, the thing to do is to find it," said Fenn, gazing closely at Alicia. "Where we find it will disclose who took it."

"I agree with you, Mr. Fenn," said a voice from the doorway, and there stood Dolly Fayre!

"Oh," cried Dotty, "I knew you wouldn't run away!"

"I did," returned Dolly, looking very sober. "I

couldn't stand things here, and I was tempted to go home."

"Did you start out with that idea?" asked Dotty.

"No; never thought of such a thing when I went out. But I took a bus that turned around and went to the station, so that made me think of Berwick and I got homesick for mother, and I just couldn't help wanting to go to her. And I telephoned back here that I was going. Then, I had no sooner done that, than it seemed to me a cowardly thing to do, after all, and I changed my mind quick and came right back here. I rode up on top of a stage, and the trip in this lovely bright air made me feel a heap better. Now then, I want to say, once for all, that I didn't take that earring, but I'm going to find out who *did*, and also I'm going to find the jewel. I don't know which I'll find first, but one means the other."

"Just what I said, Miss Fayre," exclaimed Fenn. "I'll join forces with you, and we'll see about this thing. We'll find the missing jewel and we'll find out who took it, but we'll have to put up a search."

"All my things are at your disposal," said Dolly; "look through all my cupboards and bureau drawers as you like. I'm not afraid."

"Of course not," said Fenn, "after your absence this morning! You had a fine opportunity to dispose of the jewel!"

"How dare you!" cried Dolly, turning white with rage. "I have told you truthfully where I went and why."

"Let her alone, Fenn," said Mr. Forbes, sharply. "You talk too much. Run along now, girls; we'll let the matter rest for to-day. I'll consult with Mr. Fenn, and I don't think we'll search your belongings. I can't think any one of you has intentionally concealed the jewel. It's lost but not stolen, that's what I think."

"You dear old thing!" and Bernice impulsively threw her arms around her uncle's neck. "I think you're right. But it must be found!"

"It must be found!" repeated Dolly. "Otherwise suspicion will always rest on me."

"Not on you any more than the rest of us," declared Dotty, "but there's no use in hunting any more in this room. It simply isn't here."

They had searched the room in which the jewel had been kept, thoroughly and repeatedly. So the girls went off to their own rooms to talk it all over again.

"You're too hard on them, Fenn," said Mr. Forbes to his secretary, when they were alone.

"But it's a clear case, sir. That Fayre girl took it. She got scared and tried to run home, then decided it would be better to face the music, so she returned. She's the one, of course. She adores those old trinkets; the others don't care two cents for them. She put it on her dress,— probably she took it off again, but after that the temptation to possess the thing was too strong for her. She thought you'd not miss it, and she carried it off. Then, when she was out this morning, she either threw it away, or secreted it somewhere. Perhaps she took it to some friend for safe keeping."

"I don't believe it, Fenn. I've studied the four girls pretty closely and Dolly Fayre is, I think, the most frank and honest and conscientious of them all. Why, I'd suspect either of my own nieces before I would Dolly."

"You're generous, sir. But you're mistaken. Miss Fayre is the culprit, and we'll fasten the theft on her yet."

"I hope not,— I sincerely hope not. But it's a queer business, Fenn, a very queer business."

" It's all of that, Mr. Forbes, but we'll get at the truth of it yet."

Meantime the four girls were talking over the matter. But not all together. The two D's, in their own room, and the other two girls in theirs were having separate confabs.

" Now, Dolly Fayre," Dotty was saying, " you tell me *everything* you know about this thing! I don't want any holding back or concealing of any suspicions or doubts you may have."

" It isn't really a suspicion, Dotty, but I will tell you. It's only that just as we left the room, the museum room I call it, yesterday afternoon, we were all out, and Alicia ran back. She said she had left her handkerchief on the table. And she went straight to that very table where I had laid the earring. Now, I can't suspect Alicia, but that's what she did."

" Well, Dolly," and Dotty looked thoughtful, " that's enough to cast suspicion on her. She went to that very table? "

" Yes. Of course, I didn't think anything about it at the time, but now I remember it distinctly. That's why I wanted to go home and tell Mother all about it, and ask her if I ought to tell Mr. Forbes about Alicia."

"I see. I don't know myself what you ought to do. I've been thinking it might be Alicia all the time. I hate to suspect her, as much as you do. But if she ran back, and went to that table, and then the jewel that laid there was gone, it certainly looks queer. Decidedly queer."

"Well, what shall I do?"

"I suppose you'll have to keep still, unless you're actually accused of taking it. You can't very well tell on Alicia."

"That's what I think."

"But if they really accuse you,— and Mr. Fenn has already done so."

"Oh, Fenn! I don't care what he says. If Mr. Forbes doesn't think I took it, I don't want to say anything about Alicia."

"Well, let's wait and see. After what you've just told me, I think she did take it. But I don't *want* to think that."

Now, in the next room, Alicia and Bernice were talking confidentially and in low tones.

"Of course, Dolly must have taken it," Alicia said, slowly.

"I can't believe that," said Bernice. "I know Dolly Fayre awfully well, and I just about 'most *know* she couldn't do such a thing."

"I daresay she never was tempted before. You can't tell what you may do until there's a sudden temptation. She might have thought it was no harm, when Uncle Jeff has so many of such trinkets. She might have thought he'd never miss it —"

"No," dissented Bernice. "Dolly never thought out those things. If she did take it, it was just on the spur of the moment, and, as you say, because of a sudden irresistible temptation. And the minute after she was doubtless sorry, but then she was ashamed to confess or return it."

It was luncheon time then, and the girls went downstairs together, with no disclosures of their suspicions of each other.

At the luncheon table the subject was freely discussed.

Dolly explained to Mrs. Berry that, after she had telephoned she was going home, she felt that it was a cowardly thing to do, and that she ought to remain and see the matter through.

"You see," Dolly said, smiling, "it was a sudden temptation, when I got to the station, to go home. Just the sight of the ticket office, and the train gates, gave me a wave of homesickness and I wanted to see Mother so terribly, that I thought I'd just go. But as soon as I'd telephoned, I realised that I oughtn't to do it, so I came right back here. I didn't telephone I'd changed my mind, for I thought I'd be here so soon. Mrs. Berry, what do you think became of the earring?"

"I don't know, I'm sure, my dear. I don't think I could ever believe that any one of you girls took it with any wrong intent. Did one of you just borrow it? To study it as a curio or anything like that?"

"No!" cried Bernice. "That's absurd. If I'd wanted to do that I should have asked Uncle's permission."

"Of course you would," and good Mrs. Berry sighed at the undoubted fallacy of her theory.

It was during luncheon that the telephone bell rang, and Geordie Knapp invited the girls to a matinée at the Hippodrome.

"They must come," he said to Mrs. Berry, who had answered his call. "Please let them. It's a big party. We've three boxes; my mother is going with us, and all the rest are young people. I know your girls will like it."

"Of course they will," Mrs. Berry replied. "I'll be glad to have them go. Wait; I'll ask them."

The invitation was heard with delight, and Bernice answered Geordie for the others that they'd all be glad to go.

"Good!" cried Geordie. "We'll call for you in our big car. Be ready on time."

They promised and hastened through luncheon to go to dress.

"I'm glad you're going," kind Mrs. Berry said; "it'll take your minds off this old earring business. Have a real good time, and don't even think of anything unpleasant."

So the girls started off in gay spirits, resolved not to worry over the lost jewel.

During the intermission at the matinée Dotty chanced to be talking to Geordie alone, and she told him about the mystery, and asked him what he thought. The boy was greatly interested, and asked

for all the details. So Dotty told him all, even of
Dolly's seeing Alicia return to the room and go to
the table by the window.

"Jiminy crickets!" said Geordie, "that looks
bad! But I can't believe Alicia would take it, nor
any of you others. Let me talk to Alicia; I won't
accuse her, you know, but maybe I can gather something from the way she talks."

So by changing of seats Geordie found opportunity to talk to Alicia about the matter. To his surprise, she willingly discussed it, and, moreover, she
made no secret of the fact that she suspected Dolly
of taking it. She said she felt sure that Dolly did
it, meaning no great harm, but probably being over-
tempted. "Why," said Alicia, "she said only at
luncheon that when she was at the Railroad Station
she was so tempted to go home to her mother that
she very nearly went. So, you see, she is given to
sudden temptations and I suppose she can't always
resist them."

Geordie considered. "I don't believe she took it,
Alicia," he said; "either it's slipped behind something, or else somebody else got in and took it. It
never was one of you four girls! I'm *sure* it wasn't.

If I could be over there for an hour or so, I'll bet I could find it. I'm pretty good at such things. S'pose I go home with you after the show; may I? "

" Oh, I wish you would! If you could find that thing, you would be a joy and a blessing! "

And so, after the performance was over, Geordie Knapp and Ted Hosmer both went to Mr. Forbes' house with the four girls.

Alicia asked her uncle's permission for them all to go up to the museum rooms, and he gave it. He was not entirely willing, for he rarely allowed visitors to his collections, but Alicia coaxed until he gave in.

" It can't be that Alicia took it," Dotty whispered to Dolly, " for she is so willing to have Geordie investigate."

Ted Hosmer was as anxious as Geordie to hunt for the earring, but when he reached the rooms of the collections he was so interested in looking at the specimens that he nearly forgot what they came for.

" Look at the birds! " he cried, as they passed through the Natural History room on the way to the antiques.

" You like birds? " asked Dolly, as she saw his eyes brighten at the sights all round him.

"Yes, indeed! I've a small collection myself, but nothing like this! I study about birds every chance I get. Oh, see the humming birds! Aren't they beautiful?"

But Dolly persuaded him to leave the birds and butterflies and go on to the antique room.

Here the girls told their two visitors all about the earring and its disappearance. Mr. Fenn was not present, for which Dolly was deeply grateful.

Mr. Forbes watched the two boys quizzically. Then he said,

"Go to it, Geordie. Do a little detective work. If any of my four visitors took it, make them own up. I won't scold them; I'm anxious only to know which one it was."

"You don't really think it was any of them, I know, Mr. Forbes, or you wouldn't speak like that," said Ted. "I know you think as I do, that some queer mischance or accident is responsible for the disappearance. But *what* was that accident, and *where* is the jewel?"

The two boys searched methodically. They did not look into cupboards or drawers; they asked questions and tried to think out some theory.

"Could any one have come in at the window?" asked Ted.

"No chance of that," said Mr. Forbes, "considering the window is in the fourth story, and no balcony, or any way of reaching it from the ground."

Geordie stuck his head out of the window in question.

"Who lives next door?" he said, looking across the narrow yard to the next house.

"People named Mortimer," replied Mr. Forbes. "But they're all away from home. They're somewhere down South."

"There's somebody over there. I see a light in one of the rooms."

"A caretaker, maybe. But don't be absurd. It's all of ten or twelve feet across to that house from our back extension to theirs. Are you thinking somebody could spring across, take the jewel and spring back again?"

"That *isn't* very likely, is it?" Ted laughed, "but there's some explanation, somewhere," and the boy shook his head. "You see, Mr. Forbes, somebody might have made entrance to this room after the

-{238}-

girls left it Sunday afternoon, and before you discovered your loss."

"Somebody might," agreed Mr. Forbes, "but I can't quite see how. Surely no intruder came up by way of the stairs; I can't believe any one came in by the window, and what other way is there?"

"Suppose," said Geordie, earnestly, "suppose the caretaker, or whoever is next door, saw you people examining the earring by the light from the window, — you *were* by the window, weren't you?"

"Yes," said Dolly, to whom he had put the question. "Yes, it was growing dusk, and I stepped to the window to look at the gold work."

"Well, suppose this caretaker person saw you, and realised the jewel was valuable. Then suppose after you all went out and left the earring on this little table, which is only ten or twelve inches from the window, suppose the caretaker leaned out of his window, and, with a long pole, with a hook on the end, fished the thing over to himself."

"Ridiculous!" cried Mr. Forbes. "Nobody could do such a thing as that! Absurd, my boy! Why, even a long fishpole would scarcely be long enough, and he couldn't get purchase enough on the end —"

"I admit it sounds difficult, sir, but they do pretty clever things that way."

"And, too, I can't suspect my neighbour's servants! Why, I've not the slightest cause for such suspicion!"

"Oh, no, I can't think it's that way, either," said Dolly. "Why, that caretaker is a nice old man. I've heard Mrs. Berry tell about him. His room is just opposite hers, two floors beneath this very room we're in now. He has a parrot that chatters and annoys Mrs. Berry, but the old man is honest, I'm sure. And he's too old to be agile enough to do such an acrobatic thing as you suggest."

CHAPTER XVII

A CLEVER IDEA

TED HOSMER looked at Dolly as she spoke, and a sudden light came into his eyes.

"By Jiminy!" he said, and he drew a sharp little whistle. "I say, Dolly, where is your Mrs. Berry?"

"Oh, no, Ted," Dolly laughed, "you can't connect Mrs. Berry with this matter any more than you can the Mortimers' servants. Mrs. Berry didn't do it."

"I didn't say she did," returned Ted, smiling at her. "But where is she, that's all."

"I don't know. Probably in her room."

"Take me there, will you? I must see her at once. Why, I've got an idea!"

"Goodness, Ted!" exclaimed Geordie. "What a strange piece of news!"

"Don't be funny!" said Ted; "I say, Dolly, take me to speak to Mrs. Berry, won't you?"

"Why, of course, if you like,— come on."

Dolly led the way and Ted followed. The others

paid little attention, for Geordie was thinking out a new theory of how somebody could get across from the next house, by means of scuttles to the roofs on the front part of the houses. Of course, in front the houses were attached, but the back extensions were only one room wide, thus giving ground space for tiny back yards.

A tap on Mrs. Berry's door was answered, and the two were admitted.

"What is it?" and the housekeeper looked a little surprised at her visitors.

"May we look out of your window?" asked Ted, politely.

"Surely," was the reply. "But what for?"

Ted, however, already had raised the window and was looking out. It was dark, or nearly, and the house next door showed a dim light in the room opposite the one they were in.

The shade was down at the window, so they saw nothing of the room but a few indistinct shadows.

"Tell us something about the old caretaker next door, won't you?" begged Ted, and Mrs. Berry responded: "Now, don't suspect him! Why, old Joe is the most honest man in the city! I've known him for years, and I'm sure he wouldn't steal a pin! Mr. Mortimer trusts him absolutely."

"But tell us a little about him."

"There's nothing to tell, only that he stays there alone when the family go away. He lives, practically, in the two rooms; that room opposite and the kitchen. He has no company but his parrot; he makes a great pet of that."

"A nice Polly?"

"A handsome bird, yes. But a nuisance with its continual squawking and chattering."

"Thank you, Mrs. Berry; I believe that's all. Pardon our intrusion. We'll go now. Come along, Dolly."

Dolly followed Ted from the room, and he said, "Don't go back upstairs yet. Come along with me."

"Where?"

"Never mind. Come on," and, making a gesture for her to be silent, Ted piloted her down the main staircase and out of the front door.

"Gracious! I won't go another step till you tell me where we're going!"

"Of course I'll tell you. We're going next door. Come on; you don't need wraps; it's just a step."

Taking her hand, Ted led her down the Forbes' steps and up those of the house next door. He rang the bell and they waited. In a moment, shuffling steps were heard and an old man opened the door.

" That you, Joe? " said Ted, pleasantly. " Let us come in for a moment, please."

" I don't know you, young sir, but if I'm not mistaken, this is one of the little ladies from next door."

" Quite right. We intend no harm, I assure you. Let us come in for a minute or two."

The old man let them enter and closed the door behind them.

" How's your parrot? " asked Ted, conversationally.

Old Joe looked surprised, but he answered courteously, " Polly is well, as usual."

" What kind of a bird is he? "

" A parrot, sir."

" I don't mean that. Is he honest or — or given to thievery? "

" Oh, sir, he's the thievingest beast in the world, that he is! I don't dare leave a thing around that I'm not willing for him to take if he wants it."

" Yes, just so. And does he ever go out of this house? "

" No,— oh, no."

Ted's face fell. Dolly's, too, for she began to see what Ted had in mind. But if Polly never left the Mortimer house, surely he didn't fly over and steal the earring.

" Could I go up to the room where the bird is? " said Ted, trying to conceal his disappointment at the collapse of his theory.

" Yes, sir, if you like, or I'll bring the bird down here."

" We'll go up, please," and Dolly and Ted followed the old man to the room on the second floor, which was opposite Mrs. Berry's.

They looked in and saw the bird in his cage, hanging from a bracket near the window.

" Pretty Polly," said Ted, walking toward the cage. " Nice Polly. Polly want a cracker? "

The bird cocked his head on one side, but said nothing.

" And you're sure he never leaves his cage? " said Ted, examining the fastening on the cage door.

" Well, sir, he does leave his cage. I said he

doesn't leave this house. That is,— not often. So seldom as to call it never."

"What do you mean by that?"

"Well, a few days ago,— I'm thinking it was Sunday,— the bird let himself out of his cage. The latch broke, do you see, and he could push the door open with his claw. I came into the room, and there he was stalking up and down the floor with a knowing look. I soon found how he got out of the cage and I fixed the latch so he can't do it again. I let him out often, but I'm not going to have him letting himself out."

"Sunday, was it?" and Dolly's eyes brightened as Ted went on with his questions. "And you weren't here when he got out of his cage?"

"No, sir. But I came in soon and he was marching along the floor, winking at me."

"And was the window open?"

Old Joe stopped to think. "No," he said, finally, and Dolly gave a sigh of despair. If the window had been open, there was a possibility that Polly had been the thief.

"Can he fly?" she put in.

"Fly? Yes, that he can. That's why I'm care-

ful to keep him shut up here. I wouldn't like him
to fly over and annoy Mrs. Berry. He did that once
a year ago, and the lady was right down mad about
it."

"Think again, Joe. Couldn't this window have
been open Sunday, when Polly got out of his cage?"

"Well, now, I do believe it was! Wasn't Sunday
that warm, pleasant day? Yes? Well, then, come
to think of it, this here window *was* open! My! it
was a good thing Mr. Polly didn't walk out of it!"

"But that's just what he did do,— I believe!"

"What, sir? What do you mean?"

"Well, I'll tell you. A small article has disappeared from the house next door, from a room on
this side, just above Mrs. Berry's room. It's a hard
matter to find out what became of the thing, a small
trinket of jewellery, and I'm in hopes that your bird
flew over and took it, because that will let out certain very much worried human beings!"

"Oh, I can't think Polly did that!"

"Can he fly as far as to go up to that window
two stories higher than this? You say he can fly,
but would he be likely to fly *up?*"

"If so be that window was open he might. He's

a born thief, that bird is. But in that case, what did he do with it? A jewel, you say?"

"Yes, an old, very old earring."

"Ah!" and Joe started; "of fine work, but all broken and bent?"

"I don't know. How about that, Dolly?"

"It was old, and it was fine gold work. But it wasn't bent or broken."

"Then it's not the same," said Joe. "Polly has a lot of playthings, and some old imitation jewellery that Mrs. Mortimer lets him have because he loves such things. And it was Monday, yes, yesterday, he had an old piece of stuff that I didn't remember seeing before, but I paid little attention to it. And it was that bent and twisted it can't have been the thing you're searching for. No, that it couldn't."

"I suppose not," said Ted, but Dolly said, "Let us see it, anyway, can't you? Maybe Polly bent it up himself."

Old Joe went and searched through a lot of broken bits of metal things in a box on the table.

"Here it is," he said. "You see how it's worn out!"

A CLEVER IDEA

"That's it!" cried Dolly. "Oh, Ted, *that's* the earring! Hooray!"

"Is it? Hooray!" shouted Ted. "*Really*, oh, it's too good to be true! Polly *must* have taken it, Joe."

"Yes, he must have done so, if Miss, here, says it's the one. But let me figger it out. I s'pose when Polly opened his cage door, the open window attracted him, and he flew out. Then as the other windows in the Forbes house were closed, he made for that one that was open. Was nobody in the room?"

"No," said Dolly, "not when the jewel was taken. I left it on a table, near the window, and —"

"Yes, Miss, I see! Polly was tempted by the glittering thing; he loves glitter, and he snatched it up and flew right back home with it. He hid it somewhere; that's his thievish nature, and when I came in here he was walking up and down the floor as innocent appearin' as a lamb! Oh, you wicked Polly!"

"Wick-ed Polly!" screeched the bird. "Naughty Polly!"

"Yes, very naughty Polly!" said Ted. "But a good Polly, after all, to get us out of our troubles!"

-{249}-

"Then, you see," continued Old Joe, "that villainous bird, he hid his treasure, and when I let him out yesterday, just to fly around the room, he found it out again, and he bent and broke it all up."

"Well, never mind!" Dolly cried, "as long as we have it! Oh, Ted, how clever of you to think of it! I'm so glad! Come, let's hurry home and tell about it! My, won't they all rejoice!"

"Shall I go over and make my apologies to Mr. Forbes?" asked Joe, anxiously.

"No; at least, not now. Mr. Forbes won't hold you at all to blame. It was merely coincidence that the bird happened to get out of his cage, just when the jewel lay there unprotected," said Ted.

"And, he'd taken something else if he hadn't found that. Anything glittering or sparkling catches his eye, and he steals it. But 'tis seldom he gets a chance outside the house."

"Why do you keep such a bird?" asked Dolly.

"He isn't mine. I wouldn't care to have him. He belongs to Mrs. Mortimer, and she only laughs at his thievin' traits. She thinks they're cunning. So, I must needs take good care of him. 'Twas careless of me to leave the window open, and him here

-❨250❩-

alone. But I didn't think he could break loose from his cage. I'm thinkin' the door was ajar."

" Well, we're much obliged to you and to Polly. Oh, just think if you hadn't reasoned it out, Ted, we never would have known the truth! You see, Joe thought the earring was one of Polly's own belongings, so, of course, he never would have paid any attention to it."

" That I wouldn't, Miss. I supposed it was some of the trinkets the missus gave him. She buys 'em for him at the five-and-ten. He breaks 'em as fast as he gets 'em! "

" I hope this can be straightened out, and I think it can," said Dolly, as she looked at the bent gold work.

" I'm sure it can," agreed Ted, " but anyway, it solves the mystery and clears you girls! Hooray! Hurroo!! Come on, let's go and tell them all."

The two dashed into the Forbes house next door, and found the rest of them down in the drawing room, wondering what had become of Dolly and Ted.

With a beaming face and dancing eyes, Dolly went straight to Mr. Forbes and dangled the bent and twisted earring before his surprised countenance.

"Bless my soul!" he cried, as he saw it. "Did you — where *did* you find it?"

Dolly realised that he had been about to say, "Did you decide to own up?" or something like that, and she was glad that he changed his sentence.

"Next door!" she exclaimed, for Ted stood back and let her have the pleasure of telling. "That old parrot came and stole it!"

"Oh! the parrot!" cried Mr. Forbes. "Why, of course! I see it all! Why didn't *I* think of that? Once before, I saw that bird light on my window sill, and I shooed him off. Strange I didn't think of that solution!"

"Tell us more!" cried Dotty; "who thought of a parrot? Whose parrot is it? How did he get in? When?"

"Wait a minute, Dot," said Dolly, laughing, "and I'll tell you all about it. You tell some, Ted, I'm all out of breath!"

So Ted told the whole story of their visit to the next house.

"And I thought it was n. g. when the old chap said the window in his room wasn't open. Also, when he said the bird never left that house, I thought again we were off the track. But when we went on to discuss the matter, and he said the bird was a born thief, and also he finally remembered that his window was open on Sunday afternoon, why I felt sure we had found the culprit. Then, the old fellow produced the earring, which he had seen, but had scarcely noticed, thinking it was some of the bird's own junk. It seems Polly also collects antiques!"

"Well, well, Hosmer, my boy, you did well to think of such a solution to our mystery! What put you on the track in the first place?"

"I think it was the birds of your collection, sir. I'm very fond of birds and bird study, and I know a lot about parrots, and their ways. Well, seeing all your stuffed birds, put birds in my head, I suppose; any way, when Dolly spoke of a parrot next door that annoyed Mrs. Berry, I thought right away of how that Polly bird would like to grab a gold trinket if he had a good chance. So I looked up his chances, and I began to realise that if your window was open, the one in the other house might have been too. Sunday was such a warm, pleasant day. So, I looked into matters a little, and concluded we'd better go over there. I didn't say what we were going for, because it might easily have turned out a wild goose chase —"

"Instead of a wild parrot chase!" said Alicia. "Oh, isn't it just fine that it's found!"

"I guess old Fenn will be surprised," said Dotty, with an angry shake of her dark head. "He tried his best to fasten it on Dolly —"

"Fasten the earring on?" asked Geordie Knapp, laughing.

"No; I did that myself," rejoined Dolly. "Oh, Uncle Forbes, you didn't think I took it, did you?"

"I didn't know what to think. No thought of that bird came into my mind. And so I had to cudgel my brain to think how it did disappear. For I *had* to know! Yes, I positively *had* to know!"

"Of course," agreed Bernice. "You didn't want to lose that jewel."

"It wasn't only that, there was another reason, a reason that I'll tell you some day."

CHAPTER XVIII

NEXT morning at breakfast, each of the four girls found a note at her plate. The notes were all alike, and they read:

Mr. Jefferson Forbes, because of his great delight over the discovery of his lost piece of property, invites you to a celebration occasion, to-morrow, Thursday evening. Mr. Forbes would say, also, that he has obtained the consent of all interested parents, that you may stay till Saturday. Mr. Jefferson Forbes will be glad of suggestions as to what form said celebration shall assume.

They all laughed at the formal style and stilted language of the notes, and were amazed at the information that they were to make a longer visit than they had thought.

Mrs. Berry smiled at the shower of questions that followed the reading of the notes, but she only said, "Don't ask me, my dears. After breakfast, Mr.

Forbes will meet you in the reception room and discuss it."

So a merry group of four awaited the coming of their host in the pretty little reception room.

"Good morning," he said, cheerily, as he entered, "What an attractive bunch of humanity! Four smiling faces and eight bright eyes! I greet you all."

With an old-fashioned bow, he took a seat near them, and asked, "Did you receive certain important documents?"

"We did," replied Bernice. "May we have further enlightenment?"

"You may, and first I will remove that anxious look from Dolly's face, by saying that her mother is perfectly willing that she should stay here the rest of the week."

"Oh, goody!" cried Dolly. "How did you ask her? By telephone?"

"Yes. So pleased was I over the developments of last evening, that I telephoned all the powers that be, and arranged for an extension to our house party. Are you glad?"

" Indeed we are," chorused the girls, and Uncle Jeff went on.

" Now, our celebration is to be just whatever you want. And if you don't all want the same thing, you can all have different things. So just state your preferences."

" I know mine," said Alicia. " It is to go to Muriel Brown's party on Friday night. She asked us, and I'd love to go."

" That's one," said her uncle. " Of course you can all go to the party. Now, Bernice, what do you choose? "

" I'd like to go to the opera," said Bernice. " Grand opera, I mean. I've never been but once, and I'd love to go."

" Good! We'll go to-night. If you all agree? "

They certainly did agree to that, and then Mr. Forbes asked the two D's to choose.

" I want to go to the Metropolitan Museum,— with you! " said Dolly, half afraid to ask such a boon. But Mr. Forbes seemed pleased, and declared he would be delighted to go with her, and explain the exhibits and the others could go or not, as they

liked. All decided in favour of going, and then Dotty
was asked to choose.

"Don't laugh at me," said Dotty, "but I'd like
to have a party. Only, not a big one. Just us four
girls, and the four boys, that we know the best;
Geordie, Ted, Marly Turner and Sam Graves. I
like that sort of a party better than the big, dressy
ones."

"Why, Dot Rose!" exclaimed Alicia, "I thought
you liked the big dances."

"So I do, if I knew the people. But I think it
would be lots of fun to have a few, and have a less
formal party. I'd like to ask Muriel Brown, and
two or three of those girls we met with her, the other
day, and then, have a few more boys; but not a
hundred, like Muriel had."

"A good plan," said Mr. Forbes, "because you
couldn't invite a large party on such short notice.
So, make out your list, Dotty, and invite them by
telephone at once. Mrs. Berry will help you, and
will arrange all details. Let me see, you can have
that party to-morrow night; go to the opera to-
night; go to Muriel's party on Friday night, and
go home on Saturday. The museum we can visit any

afternoon. I thank you for your kind attention."

"Oh, Uncle Jeff, we thank *you* for your kindness, all of it," cried Alicia. "You have been so very good to us, and now you are doing a lot more for our pleasure."

"Have you enjoyed it all, so far, Alicia?" and her uncle looked at her inquiringly.

"Oh, yes, sir, indeed I have! I was troubled about the lost earring, but that was not your fault."

"Nor the fault of any of you girls," said Mr. Forbes. "As I have hinted to you, I have a reason for this visit you are making me, beside a desire to give you pleasure. I am considering a serious matter and this stay of yours in my house is helping me to a decision."

"What can it be, Uncle?" cried Bernice. "Tell us, so we can help you more, and more intelligently."

"I will tell you Saturday morning," he returned with a smile. "Perhaps in that time other developments may occur that will alter my final decision in the matter."

"It sounds most mysterious," laughed Dolly, "can't we guess what it's all about?"

"You may guess, if you like, but I don't promise

to tell you if you guess correctly. And I don't mind adding, that I feel pretty sure you couldn't guess correctly, if you tried!"

"No use trying, then!" said Alicia, gaily. "Oh, I'm so glad we're going to stay longer. I want to do a lot of things beside the celebrations we've just planned. I do think you're the best and kindest uncle in the whole world! I've got a secret, too, and some day I'm going to tell it to you all."

"Secrets seem to be the order of the day," laughed Dolly; "we'll have to scrape up one, Dot."

"Well, it's no secret that we're having one grand, glorious, good time!" said Dotty. "What's on for this morning?"

Mr. Forbes went off to his own room then, and the girls planned out all they should do for the rest of their stay in the city.

There was some shopping, some sight-seeing and some errands yet undone but they at last agreed on a programme that would suit everybody.

Dotty's party, as they called it, took place on Thursday night, and she had her way about having it a small gathering. There were about twenty in all,

FOUR CELEBRATIONS

and according to Dotty's wishes it was not only a
dancing party.   There were games as well as dances,
for Dotty loved games.

Some of the city young people were at first inclined to laugh at the idea of games, but when they
began to take part in these that Dotty had planned
they became exceedingly interested.

One was an " Observation Test," up in Mr. Forbes'
museum.

At Dotty's request, he had allowed the collection
rooms to be opened to the guests, and this very special dispensation was so appreciated by all that they
were most exceedingly careful not to handle the rare
specimens or touch the exhibits.

This state of things lent itself beautifully to the
game.   Each player was asked to walk about for
half an hour and look at the curios and treasures,
and at the expiration of the time, to return to the
drawing room, and spend ten minutes writing down
the names of such objects as could be remembered.

This game, most of them had played before, with
a table full of less interesting exhibits.   But in the
wonderful museum rooms of Mr. Forbes it was quite
another story.

So eagerly did the young people observe and examine the things, that the half hour allotted for that purpose slipped away all too soon.

And then they sat down to write their lists, and that too proved an absorbing occupation.

Our four girls wrote lists, just for fun, but did not compete for the prizes, as, knowing the exhibits so well, that would not have been fair.

Muriel Brown took the first prize, and the hostesses were glad of it for it was pleasant to have Muriel so honoured.

The prize was a gold penholder, and the boys' prize, which Marly Turner won, was a similar gift.

After it was over, another game was played. This was ribbon cutting.

Girls and boys, stood at either end of the long drawing-room. To each girl was given the end of a piece of long, narrow ribbon, and a pair of scissors. The other end of each ribbon was held by a boy, who likewise had a pair of scissors.

At a signal, each player started cutting the ribbon straight through the middle. If the scissors slipped and cut through the selvage, the player was out of the game. It was not easy, for the ribbon was narrow, and there was a strong impulse to hurry, which made for crooked cutting. The middle of each piece of ribbon was marked by a knot, and whoever reached the knot first, was the winner of that pair. The one who finished first of all, received a special prize.

The game caused great laughter and sport, and the city young people declared they enjoyed it quite as much as dancing.

Then the feast was served, and very beautiful and elaborate it was. The celebration, Mr. Forbes had said, was to be especially for the two D's, as it was Dotty's choice, and Dolly's choice of a visit to the museum provided little opportunity for gaiety.

The table showed two great floral D's, one at either end. Dotty's was made of red roses, and Dolly's of pink roses. Every guest had as a souvenir, some pretty and valuable little trinket, and at every place was a small D made of flowers.

Cakes, ices, jellies, and all such things as could be so shaped, were cut in the form of D's, and our two girls felt greatly honoured to see their initial so prominently and beautifully displayed.

In the centre of the table was a huge French Doll,

of the finest type. It was dressed in silk covered with polka dots, and its hat and parasol were of silk to match.

Everybody laughed when Mr. Forbes pointed out that it was Dotty Dolly! And all agreed it was a most clever and appropriate symbol.

After supper there was dancing, and a fine orchestra furnished the music. Our girls liked dancing pretty well, but often they sat out a dance talking to one or another of their guests.

Once, as Dolly passed along the hall, chatting with Geordie Knapp, they heard rather loud voices behind the closed door of the little reception room.

Rather surprised that the door should be shut at all, that evening, Dolly paused involuntarily, and Geordie stood by her side. They had no intention of eavesdropping; indeed, Geordie thought perhaps some new game was about to be announced.

But to Dolly's amazement, she heard Alicia's voice saying, " Oh, I cannot! I dare not! "

The tones were quivering with emotion, and Dolly couldn't help listening for the next words. She feared Alicia was troubled about something; indeed, she didn't know what she feared.

And, next came a voice that was unmistakably Marly Turner's, saying, "Do, dear! Oh, *trust* me, — *I* will take care of you!"

"But it is a desperate step!" exclaimed Alicia, "if I should ever regret it!"

"You will not regret it, dearest," Marly said, "I will never *let* you regret it! Your own mother eloped; it is fitting you should do so, too."

Dolly looked at Geordie, her face white with horror.

Alicia, planning an elopement! And with Marly Turner! She laid her hand on the knob of the door.

"Don't!" said Geordie, "don't you get mixed up in a thing like that! Is Alicia Steele that sort of a girl?"

"I don't know," faltered Dolly. "I heard Bernice hint once that Alicia's mother did elope with her father,— but, Alicia! Why, she isn't seventeen, yet!"

"Well, that's old enough to know what she's about. I advise you, Dolly, not to go in there. Tell Mr. Forbes, if you like."

"Oh, I couldn't tell on Alicia!"

And, then, as they still stood there, too fascinated

to move away, Alicia said, " Yes, to-morrow night. I will steal out after the house is quiet,— oh, my hero! my idol!"

" My angel!" exclaimed Marly, in a deep, thrilled voice, and Dolly turned away, sick at heart.

" I don't know what to do!" she said to Geordie, as they went on to the drawing room, where the dancers were.

" Don't do anything," he advised. " It's none of your business. That Steele girl isn't like you, she's a different type. If she wants to cut up such didoes, don't you mix in it. Let her alone. I knew Marly liked her,— he said so,— but I didn't suppose he'd do such a thing as that! But I shan't say a word to him. We're good friends, but not chums. Marly's a good chap, but he's awfully anxious to act grown up, and my stars! he's doing so! Elope with the Steele girl! Jiminy!"

" I can't bear to tell on Alicia," said Dolly, " and yet, I can't think I ought to let her go ahead and do this thing. She's so fond of romance, and excitement, she doesn't realise what she's doing."

Later on, Dolly saw Alicia and young Turner emerge from the reception room, and saunter toward the drawing room. They were talking earnestly, in whispers. Alicia's cheeks were pink, and her manner a little excited. Marly looked important, and bore himself with a more grown up air than usual.

Dolly and Geordie looked at each other, and shook their heads. It was only too evident that the two were planning some secret doings. They went off by themselves and sat on a davenport in a corner of the room, and continued to converse in whispers, oblivious to all about them.

Dolly and Geordie purposely walked past the other pair, and distinctly heard Marly say something about a rope ladder.

" It's part of the performance," he urged, as Alicia seemed to demur.

Then she smiled sweetly at him, and said, " All right, then, just as you say."

" It's perfectly awful! " said Dolly, as they walked on. " I've simply got to tell Dotty, anyway."

" Oh, I wouldn't," expostulated Geordie; " I don't believe they'll pull it off. Somebody will catch on and put a stop to it."

" Maybe and maybe not," said Dolly, dubiously. " Alicia is awfully clever, and if she sets out to do a thing, she generally carries it through. And her head is full of crazy, romantic thoughts. She'd rather elope than to go back to school, I know she would. She told me she'd do anything to get out of going back to school."

"That makes it look serious," agreed Geordie. "Still I don't think you ought to mix yourself up in it, unless you just tell the whole story to Mr. Forbes."

"I hate to be a tattle-tale," and Dolly looked scornful. "But if it's for Alicia's good, maybe I ought to."

"Look at them now! Their heads close together, and whispering like everything!"

"Yes, they're planning for their getaway!"

During the rest of the evening, Dolly watched Alicia, feeling mean to do it, and yet unable to keep herself from it.

At last the guests went home, one and all exclaiming at the good time they had had. Marly Turner bade Dolly good night, with a smiling face. "I've had the time of my life!" he declared.

"I've not seen much of you," said Dolly, pointedly.

"I know it. Too bad! I wanted to dance with you oftener, but the time was so short."

" And you found another charmer? "

" Well, Alicia sure is a wonder, isn't she? You know she is! "

" Yes, she is," said Dolly, and for the life of her, she couldn't frown on the happy-hearted youth.

Marly went off, and the others followed.

" I'm not going to talk things over to-night," said Dolly, when the four were alone. " I'm tired, and I'm going straight to bed."

CHAPTER XIX

ALICIA'S SECRET

THE time seemed fairly to fly. Each of the four girls had some last few errands to do, each wanted some little souvenirs for herself, or for her people at home, and so busy were they that there was not so much mutual conversation among them as usual.

They were to go home on Saturday. And already it was Friday afternoon. They had finished luncheon, Alicia and Bernice had gone to their room, and Dolly was about to go upstairs, when she remembered that she had planned to run in and say goodbye to old Joe and his parrot.

Dolly felt she owed a debt of gratitude to Polly, and she had bought a little toy for him.

"I'm going to run in next door a minute," she said to Mrs. Berry.

"Very well, my dear. Here's a cracker for Polly."

Dolly took it laughingly, and went out to the hall.

"Put your coat round you," called out Mrs. Berry. "It's only a step, I know, but it's a very cold day."

"Oh, Dot just took my coat upstairs, with her own. Well, here's Alicia's hanging on the hall rack. I'll throw this round me."

She did so, and ran out of the front door and up the steps of the next house.

Old Joe answered her ring at the bell.

"Just ran over to say good-bye," laughed Dolly, "and to bring a cracker and a toy for Polly."

"Thank you, Miss," and Joe smiled at her. "I'll bring the bird down to you, Ma'am, to save your going upstairs."

"All right," said Dolly, a little absent-mindedly, for she was thinking of a lot of things at once.

Still absentmindedly, she put her hand in her coat pocket for a handkerchief. There was none there, and she drew out a letter instead. Then she suddenly remembered she had on Alicia's coat, and with a glance at the envelope, she thrust the letter back in the pocket. But that one glance sufficed to show her it was in Marly Turner's handwriting.

She had had a note from him a day or two ago,

inviting her to some party or other, and his striking, sprawling penmanship was unmistakable. The letter had been opened, and Dolly remembered that Alicia had had several letters in the mail that morning.

It all recalled to her the talk she had overheard the night before. All that morning Alicia had seemed preoccupied, and twice she had gone off by herself to telephone in a booth, which the girls rarely used, for they had no secrets from one another.

Dolly thought over the situation between Alicia and young Turner. She had not told Dotty yet. She had two minds about doing so. It seemed to her one minute that she had no right to interfere in Alicia's affairs and then again, it seemed as if she ought to tell Mr. Forbes what was going on.

She had heard Alicia say to Marly that they would elope that very night, and she felt sure they meant to do so.

They were all going to Muriel Brown's party, that being Alicia's own choice of the "celebrations." Would she elope from the party, or return home first? The latter, probably, for they had mentioned a rope ladder, and that seemed as if Alicia meant to go late at night when all the others were asleep. If she ran away from the party there would be no need of a rope ladder.

Dolly had asked Bernice if Alicia's mother had eloped, and Bernice had said she thought she had, though she had never heard any of the particulars.

And then Joe came down with the parrot, and Dolly forgot Alicia and her elopement for the moment.

Polly showed great delight over his gifts, and after a few words of good-bye to the bird and to old Joe, Dolly ran back again.

In the hall she took off Alicia's coat and hung it on the rack just as Alicia herself appeared on the stairs.

" Where you been? " she called out gaily.

" Next door," said Dolly, " to say a fond farewell to Polly Mortimer. And as my coat was upstairs, I took the liberty of wearing yours."

" That's all right," laughed Alicia, " you're welcome to it, I'm sure. Oh, I say, Dolly, there's a letter in the pocket of it! I hope you didn't read it!"

" Alicia Steele! You ought to be ashamed of yourself to hint at such a thing!"

"There, there, don't flare up over nothing! I only said I hoped you didn't. Did you?"

"I consider that question insulting!"

"Yes, people often get out of answering, that way! Now, you haven't answered me yet. Did you or did you *not* read that letter that's in the pocket of my coat?"

"I did *not!* But I've my opinion of a girl who could even think I'd do such a thing!"

"Well, you had plenty of time, and when you were in next door, would have been a good opportunity. I'm not sure I believe you even yet. You're blushing like fury!"

"Who wouldn't, at being insulted like that! I don't think you can have much sense of honour yourself, to think anybody decent would read another person's letter!"

"Now, don't get huffy, little goldilocks!" and Alicia laughed at her. "I had to be sure, you see, because it's a most important matter, and I wouldn't have anybody know for the world,— until I get ready to tell, myself."

"And when will you be ready to tell?" Dolly

tried to speak lightly, but the words nearly choked her.

"I dunno. Maybe you'll know about it to-morrow."

"Oh, Alicia —" Dolly meant to speak a word of warning or of pleading, indeed she didn't quite know what she *was* going to say, but just then, Dotty and Bernice came down stairs, and proposed they all go for a motor ride, and a last visit to the pretty tea-room.

Dolly agreed, but Alicia didn't seem quite willing.

"I'm expecting a telephone message," she said, at last. "You girls go on, and leave me at home. I shan't mind."

"Oh, no," said Dotty, "we four can't be together after to-day. We mustn't be separated this last day of all. Come on, 'Licia."

"But it's an important message," and Alicia looked anxious.

"Can I be of help?" said Mrs. Berry, coming toward them.

"Yes," cried Dotty, "let Mrs. Berry take the message, and tell her what answer to make."

"No answer," said Alicia, slowly, and a pink flush rose to her cheeks. "But just take the message, if you please, dear Mrs. Berry. It will be short, I know. Jot it down, lest you forget the exact wording."

Mrs. Berry promised and the four ran away to get ready for their last afternoon together.

"Dress up pretty, girls," Alicia called from her room. "No telling whom we might meet at the tearoom."

"That's so," said Dotty; "put on your Dresden silk, Doll."

Dolly laughingly agreed, and the four dressed-up young ladies started off.

A few calls at various shops, a few stops to look once more at certain points of interest they admired, and then for a long drive through the parks, and finally to the tearoom.

"How short the time has been," said Bernice, as they flew along.

"Yes," assented Alicia, "it doesn't seem possible we've been here as long as we have. Oh, I don't want to go home. I wish I could live in New York, I just love it!"

"I like it," said Dolly, "but I don't want to live here. I'd *like* to come here oftener than I do, though."

At the tearoom they found Janet Knapp and Corinne Bell, two girls whom they had come to know very pleasantly.

"Sit here with us," called out Janet, as they entered. "We haven't ordered yet,— what do you girls want?"

"Café frappé for me," said Dotty, "and waffles."

"Thick chocolate and whipped cream for mine," said Alicia. "Oh, when shall I ever get these lovely things again? Think of going back to boarding-school diet!"

"Don't you have good things to eat at that nice school?" asked Dolly.

"Oh, good enough, but not lovely, fancy things like these."

"I'd like to go to boarding-school," said Janet, "but mother doesn't want me away from home. She thinks girls get no home training at those fashionable schools."

"We don't, and that's a fact," admitted Alicia. "We're taught manners and, oh, well, I s'pose it's up to the girl herself, as to what she learns. Maybe I won't go back to school, after all."

" Oh, Alicia," cried Bernice, " what do you mean? "

" Oh, nothing," and Alicia smiled as she tossed her head. " I've got a secret. I can't tell you now. Maybe you'll know soon."

Dolly looked at Alicia, in bewilderment. Could she be referring to her intended elopement with Marly Turner?

" Good gracious! What do you mean? " and Janet laughed.

" Never mind," returned Alicia, airily, " don't ask me any questions. You know they call me ' that awful Alicia!' So be prepared for anything."

Dolly grew thoughtful. Only she and Geordie Knapp held the secret of Alicia's strange remarks, and she couldn't decide whether it was her duty to tell anyone of her knowledge or not. She made up her mind to tell Mrs. Berry, as soon as she went home, and then she had compunctions about that, for Dolly was very conscientious and she really didn't know what was right to do.

" I go to an awfully nice school," Corinne Bell said. " It's quite near my house and I can go alone every day. We have such interesting teachers, and such a jolly lot of girls. You'd love it, Alicia."

"Yes, I'd love it, but how could I go there? It isn't a boarding school, is it?"

"No; but couldn't you board somewhere in New York?"

"Alone! No, I should say not! You know I live out in the western wilds, at least the middle western wilds, and I think they're wilder than the far west. This little New York visit is all poor Alicia will see of the glittering metropolis for,— oh, well, it may be for years and it may be forever!"

"What do you do in vacation time?" asked Janet.

"Oh, Dad and I go to summery places. Couldn't come to New York then, you know. But when I get married, I'm going to live in New York, you can bet on that!"

"You're not thinking of marrying soon, I hope," and Janet laughed.

"Never can tell!" said Alicia, smiling saucily. "I have all sorts of wonderful schemes in my noddle. Some of 'em materialise,— some don't. But trust little Alicia to do something big! Oh, girls, my secret is just *too* splendid!"

" Is it — is it all right? " and Dolly stammered, as she looked at Alicia with a doubtful glance.

" Is it all right! You little sanctimonious-eyed prude! You bet it's all right! Maybe we'll meet again, Janet. You can't 'most always sometimes tell."

" I hope you'll come to Berwick to visit me, Alicia," said Bernice; " I think as we're cousins we ought to see more of each other."

" I'd love to, Bernie. Maybe I'll come this summer."

" We could have a sort of reunion at our house," went on Bernice; " Muriel and you girls could come for a few days, and the two D's and I would be there, and we'd scare up a lot of fun."

" 'Deed we would! I'll surely come if it can be arranged. But I never know Dad's plans from one day to the next," Alicia said.

" Hello, girls," sang out a boyish voice, and in came Geordie Knapp with half a dozen comrades. " We just sorter, kinder thought we'd see a bunch of peaches here about this time o' day! Hello, everybody ! "

Marly Turner was not among the group, and

Dolly looked anxiously at Geordie, as if to ask him what he knew concerning him.

" What is it, Dolly? " asked Geordie, with a blank look.

" Secret! " laughed Dolly, " come over here and whisper to me."

" Oh, how rude! " cried Alicia; " even out West we don't whisper in polite society! "

" But this is a special case," and Dolly smiled and dimpled, as if about to discuss the most trivial subject with Geordie.

The boy looked surprised when Dolly spoke to him about what they had overheard the night before.

" Why," he said, " I never gave it another thought! I don't believe they really meant what we thought they did."

" Yes, they did," asserted Dolly. " All day, Alicia has been keyed up to some great excitement. She had a letter from Marly this morning, and she expects a telephone from him. Also, she said things that could only mean that they really are going to elope to-night."

" Such as what? "

" She said maybe she'd live in New York soon,

and said she had a big, wonderful secret and we'd know it to-morrow,— why, she even said she expects to live in New York after she's married!"

"Whew! that's going some! Still, Dolly, I don't just see what we can do."

"I think I ought to tell Mr. Forbes, don't you?"

"I don't know. I do hate tell other people's secrets."

"Yes; so do I. Perhaps I'll just tell Mrs. Berry."

"I say, I've an idea! Suppose I get hold of Turner, and get him to go home and spend the evening with me. I'll insist upon it, you know, and if he objects, I'll ask him what's up."

"Oh, yes, Geordie, that will be fine! You do that, will you?"

"Yes; suppose I telephone him now, and ask him."

"Go ahead, and then tell me what he says."

Geordie excused himself and went off to the telephone booth.

"You seem to have a lot of secrets, too, Dolly," said Alicia.

"Yes, I have," and Dolly looked demure. "Can't let you have all the fun, 'Licia."

" Nothing doing," Geordie reported to Dolly, as he came back, and his face looked more serious. He made an opportunity to speak to her alone again, and he said, " I got him all right, and he said he couldn't see me this evening, for he's awful busy. Said he was busy with his father."

" His father! Why, Mr. Turner is an actor, isn't he? "

" Sure he is, one of the best."

" Then how can Marly be with him? Isn't Mr. Turner acting? "

" Not just now. He's rehearsing, I think."

" Well, I believe Marly made that up. He's planning the elopement."

" I'm afraid he is. He was sort of queer and didn't answer as straightforwardly as he usually does. Oh, what a silly performance to cut up! Why, they're just a couple of kids! "

" I know it. I never was mixed up in a thing like this before."

" You're not mixed up in this."

" No; not unless I mix in purposely. And I believe I shall have to. You see, I'm only a country girl, and I don't know what's right to do in this case.

-{283}-

But I'm going to follow my instinct, and tell either Mr. Forbes or Mrs. Berry. I don't think I'll tell Dot or Bernice, for they'd have no more knowledge of what's right to do, than I have myself."

"You're a good deal of a trump, Dolly Fayre. But I think you're in a hard place. I wish I could help you, and I'll do anything you say."

"Couldn't you go to Mr. Turner?"

"I'd hate to. Yer see, us fellows don't tell on each other,— it isn't done —"

"I know. Well, let's hope we're mistaken."

"But I don't see how we can be,— after what we heard."

"Neither do I. I've a mind to speak straight out to Alicia about it."

"Do, if you think best."

"Well, I'll see."

CHAPTER XX

STILL uncertain what she'd do, Dolly went home with the rest of the quartette.

Alicia was in high spirits, constantly exclaiming, "Oh, if you only knew what I know!" or "I'm terribly excited over my secret! Just you wait till to-morrow!" or some such speech.

And as they entered the Forbes house she flew to Mrs. Berry demanding to know if a telephone message had arrived for her.

"Yes," replied the good-natured housekeeper. "Marly Turner called up, and he asked me to tell you that everything was all right, and he'd pull it off to-night, sure."

"Oh, goody!" cried Alicia, "are you sure that's just what he said?"

"Yes," asseverated Mrs. Berry, "see, I wrote it down, so I shouldn't forget."

Dolly had to eavesdrop a little to overhear this

conversation, as Alicia had drawn Mrs. Berry aside, to make her inquiries. And it was with a heavy heart that Dolly went upstairs to lay off her wraps.

"Oh, girls, I'm so happy!" cried Alicia, as she flung herself into a chair. "But don't ask me why, for I refuse to tell you. Now, do we dress for to-night's party before dinner or after?"

"Before, please," said Mrs. Berry, who had followed the girls to their rooms. "Mr. Forbes asked me to tell you that he wants an interview in the drawing-room before you go to Muriel's, and so you'd better be dressed."

"Ah, those drawing-room interviews!" exclaimed Bernice. "How they frightened me at first; then they rather bored me; but in the last few days I've come to like them!"

"So have I," said Dotty. "I like Mr. Forbes himself a whole lot better than I did at first. He's so much more get-at-able."

"He ought to be," laughed Alicia, "with four girls to train him up in the way he should go! What frocks, ladies? Our very bestest?"

"Yes, indeed," said Bernice. "This is our last night, and we must 'go out in a blaze of glory'!

And scoot, you two D's. We've none too much time to dress."

Dolly and Dotty went to their room, and it was rather a silent Dolly who sat down to the dressing-table to brush her golden locks.

" Whatamatter, Dollums? " said her chum. " Sad at thoughts of going home? "

" Oh, no; really, Dot, I'm glad to go home. We've had a magnificent time here, but I'm — well, I s'pect I'm homesick."

" So'm I, a little, now that you mention it. But we've enough to remember and think over for a long time, haven't we? "

" Of course. My but I'm glad that earring was found! Oh, Dot, wouldn't it have been awful if we had gone home with that doubt hanging over us? "

" It would, indeed, old girl. And, now if you'll proceed to do up that taffy-coloured mass on top of your head, I'll accept the dressing mirror for a while."

Dolly twisted up her golden mop, and decorated it with a ribbon band, and then gave over her place to Dotty.

And, shortly, four very much dressed-up girls

went down to the extra elaborate dinner that was served in honour of the last night of their visit.

The chat at table was far more gay and spontaneous than it had been on the night of their arrival, for all had become used to each other's ways, and had grown to like each other very much. Mr. Forbes, too, had changed from a stiff, somewhat embarrassed host to a genial, even gay comrade. He asked all about their doings of the day, and they told him, with gay stories of funny episodes.

Dolly watched Alicia, but except that her eyes were unusually bright and her laughter very frequent, the Western girl showed no especial excitement.

After dinner they all went to the drawing-room, and it was with a feeling of real sadness that Dolly realised it was for the last time.

Mr. Forbes walked up and down the room as he often did, and then paused in front of the group of girls who were standing by the piano.

" Sit down, girlies," he said; " Alicia and Bernice, sit on that sofa, please,— you two D's on that one."

Uncle Jeff was smiling, but still, there seemed to be an undercurrent of seriousness in his tone, that implied a special talk.

"Did it ever occur to any of you," he began, "that I invited you here for something beside a mere desire to give you young people some pleasure?"

"Why, you've practically said so to us, Uncle Jeff," laughed Alicia; "are you going to tell us your reason?"

"Yes, I am. And I'm going to tell you now."

Mr. Forbes sat down in an easy chair, in such a position that he could look straight at all the girls, but his gaze rested on his two nieces.

"My reason," he said, slowly, "is, I admit, a selfish one. If you girls have enjoyed your visit, I'm very glad, but what I wanted, was to study you."

"I knew it!" exclaimed Bernice. "I thought you were studying us — our characters."

"Yes, just that. And I wanted to study the characters of my two nieces. Now you know you can't judge much of girls, unless you see them with their comrades, their chums; or at least with other girls of their own age. So I asked you each to bring a girl friend with you. As it happened, Bernie brought two, and Alicia none, but that didn't matter. And

I'm exceedingly glad to have met and known the two D's."

The courteous old gentleman bowed to Dotty and Dolly who smiled and bowed in return.

"Well," Uncle Jeff went on, "here's the reason I wanted to study my two nieces. Because I want to take one of them to live with me, and to inherit, eventually, my house and the greater part of my fortune."

There was a silence, as each of his hearers thought over what this would mean.

Either Bernice or Alicia was to be chosen to live in that big city house, practically to be mistress of it, to have a life of wealth and luxury and at last to inherit Mr. Forbes' great fortune, and all his valuable collections and belongings.

Dotty broke the silence. "It's great!" she exclaimed, "just great! And which one are you going to choose?"

"I have chosen," said Mr. Forbes, slowly, "it remains to be seen whether the one I have selected will accept. But now, you all can see why I was so alarmed and anxious over the episode of the lost earring. I *had* to find out if any of you girls had yielded to temptation. And if so, if it was one of my nieces, or one of their friends."

"And if it had been one of your nieces, you would have chosen the other!" cried Bernice.

"No, my child," returned her uncle. "Quite the contrary. If either you or Alicia had taken that gem, with a wrong intent, I should have asked the wrong-doer to come and live with me, hoping I could teach her the error of her ways. But that's neither here nor there. For none of you *did* take the jewel, nor indeed, ever thought of such a thing. But my decision, which I have made, is not entirely based on worthiness, or even on desirability. And I'll tell you frankly, had I tried to choose my favourite between Bernie and 'Licia, I should have had a hard time! For I have come to love both girls very dearly, and would have not the slightest objection to adopting them both."

"And us two also?" asked Dotty, mischievously.

"Yes, and you two also! Bless my soul! From a lonely, somewhat misanthropic old man, you young people have turned me into a real human being! I like young voices round me, and young folks's pleasures going on in my house. Well, my dears, are you interested to know my choice?"

"*Are* we?" cried Dotty, while Dolly fairly held her breath.

"I have chosen Alicia," Mr. Forbes announced, and there was a deep silence.

Bernice looked a little bewildered, but not at all disappointed. Alicia looked simply stunned, and the two D's just listened for further developments.

"But don't you for one minute think," said Mr. Forbes, "that I consider Alicia in any way superior to Bernice; nor, on the other hand, do I think Bernie better than Alicia. I love my nieces equally, and the thing that settled the question in my mind was a letter I received to-day from Alicia's father."

"I know!" cried Alicia, "I had one, too. I didn't say anything about it, because Dad asked me not to. You tell, Uncle Jeff."

"It's this," said Mr. Forbes. "Alicia's father is to be married soon. As you know, Alicia's mother, my dear sister died many years ago, and I know Mr Steele but slightly. However, now that he is about to remarry, I hope that it will please both him and his new wife if Alicia comes to live with me. Also, I hope it will please Alicia."

"Oh, Uncle Jeff!" and Alicia flew over to him, and flung her arms round his neck, "indeed it does please me! Why, only to-day I was saying how I'd *love* to live in New York, and how I *hated* to go back to that old school! But I never dreamed of such a thing as this!"

"Oh, it's just fine!" exclaimed Bernice. "I couldn't think of leaving father, and I'd rather live in the country anyhow —"

"I discovered that, Bernie, girl," said her uncle, seriously. "That's why I had you girls here, so I could see for myself what your tastes and traits really are. I've learned that Bernice prefers her own home and too that she doesn't want to leave her father alone though my plan would have been if I asked Bernice to come here to have her father live here, too. However, I also discovered that Alicia is unhappy in her school life, that she does not care much about returning to her Western home to live with a stepmother, and that she adores New York City! So, I wrote to her father asking his opinion, and he leaves the settlement of the question to Alicia, herself."

" And I settle it! Yes! oh, I certainly *do!* " and the girl gave her kind uncle another big embrace.

" Isn't it funny you should have been saying to-day that perhaps you might live in New York? " said Bernice.

" Yes," replied Alicia, and her face changed, " but I didn't mean *this!* "

Dolly spoke impulsively. In fact, it seemed as if she couldn't keep still.

" Suppose you tell your uncle just what you *did* mean," she said, looking straight at Alicia with an unmistakably meaning gaze.

Alicia turned on her with a sudden expression of anger.

" You *did* read that note in my coat pocket! " she cried, " you *did* read it, Dolly Fayre! and you pretended you were too honourable to do such a thing! "

" Why, Alicia, I did not! You take that back! "

" Bless my soul! Are you two quarrelling? What *is* the matter? "

" Dolly read my note! " cried Alicia, " she —"

" I did not! " interrupted Dolly, her blue eyes

blazing. "Alicia has a secret, and I think she ought to tell it!"

"I've got a right to have a secret if I like,— Dolly Fayre!"

"But it isn't a nice secret! You wouldn't want Uncle Forbes to know it! It's — it's shocking!"

"How do *you* know?"

"I know all about it,— at least I know something about it. I heard you and Marly Turner —"

"Oh, pshaw! you little blue-eyed goose! You only think it's shocking, because you're so prim and straight-laced! I'll tell Uncle Jeff, myself, and I'll tell him right now!"

"All right, Alicia," and Dolly drew a big sigh of relief. If Alicia would tell her own secret, it would take all responsibility from her shoulders.

But Alicia hesitated. She began to speak once or twice, and stammered and paused.

At last she said, "I hate to tell, it sounds so — so grown-up and ambitious."

"I should think it *did!*" cried Dolly, who began to wonder if Alicia were crazy.

"You tell him, Dolly," and Alicia suddenly looked very shy and embarrassed.

" Do you *mean* it? Do you want *me* to tell him? "

" Yes, I honestly wish you would. Though how you found out about it, I don't see! "

" We weren't intending to listen, Alicia, but Geordie Knapp and I heard you and Marly Turner, in the little reception-room last night."

" Oh, that explains it! Yes, we did talk pretty loud. Well, what did you think of it, Dolly? "

" If you say so, I'll tell the rest, and see what they think of it."

" All right, go ahead! Spare my blushes, good people, but I am fearfully embarrassed! "

Everybody looked uncomprehending, and Dolly began.

She couldn't see how Alicia could treat the matter so lightly, but was fervently thankful that she did so.

" It's this," said Dolly, solemnly, " Alicia is planning to elope with Marly Turner."

There were four astonished faces that greeted this announcement, but none showed such blank amazement as Alicia's own.

" Oh, Dolly! " she cried. " Oh, Dolly Fayre! You will be the death of me yet! Go on, tell them more! "

" That's about all I know. They planned it last

night and it just happened that Geordie and I heard them. Marly coaxed her, and Alicia hesitated and then consented. She said her mother eloped, and she would do the same. They were going to have a rope ladder."

"Oh, Dolly! Oh, Uncle Jeff! Oh, Dollyrinda!"

"Well, Alicia, suppose you stop yelling, oh, and tell me about this interesting performance," Mr. Forbes spoke, severely.

But Alicia had thrown herself into a big chair and was screaming with laughter. Every time she essayed to speak, she went off in uncontrollable spasms of mirth and when she wiped her eyes and endeavoured to speak, she giggled again.

Dolly realised there was some misunderstanding somewhere and waited for the explanation.

At last it came.

"No, Uncle Jeff," and Alicia managed to speak intelligibly, "I'm not going to elope with Marly or anybody else. I'm going to live here with you."

"But you were!" said Dolly. "You planned to!"

"No, my child," and Alicia laughed again. "I'll have to tell my story myself. I've written a play,

Uncle, and in it, the heroine elopes with the handsome hero. I was awfully shy about showing it to anybody, but Marly said he'd try to persuade his father to read it over and see if it showed any promise. You know it's a great thing to have Mr. Turner read your play, and I was delighted. Well, last night, Marly and I went over the elopement scene, that's the strong act of the play, and that's what Dolly heard, and she thought we were talking ourselves! Oh, Dolly, if people plan to elope they don't do it at the top of their lungs! Marly and I read the various character parts to see how it would sound in different voices. Well, then, he said he'd try to get his father to read it to-night, so I'd know before I went away to-morrow. And he telephoned that he'd pull it off,— he meant he'd get his father to read it. That's my secret. And, you know, Uncle Jeff, my mother *did* elope, because her father didn't want her to marry Jim Steele. And I'd heard the story of her elopement so often, and it was so dramatic, that I put it in my play. Oh, Dolly, what a little innocent you are!"

"I don't care if I am," returned Dolly, and her pretty face beamed with smiles. "I think your secret is lovely, Alicia, and I think Uncle Forbes' secret is too."

" So do I," said Dotty, " and I'm glad and proud that Dollyrinda and I are chums of two such talented and distinguished girls."

" And *I'm* glad, Alicia," said her uncle, " that you have a taste for writing. I shall be glad to help you cultivate it and I've no doubt that Mr. Turner can give you valuable advice. Of course your early efforts can't amount to much, but if you care to keep at it, you may yet do good work. Well, then, do I understand, that you accept my invitation to live with me? "

" Yes, indeed, you dear, darling old uncle! I'll live with thee, and be thy love! as the poet sings."

" Then run away to your party now, and we'll settle all further details to-morrow."

" And you'll forgive me, Alicia, for misjudging you? " said Dolly, still smiling at her funny mistake.

" Yes, indeed, you blue-eyed angel! And you'll forgive me for thinking you read my note. In it, Marly said he thought he could get his father to read my manuscript and I was *so* excited over it. But of course I know you wouldn't touch my letter only I was so upset over it, I hardly knew what I said."

"Oh, that's all right. And, girls, won't we have the great times having Alicia come to Berwick to see us all?"

"Yes, and having you all come here to visit me!" returned Alicia.

"We'll always be chums," said Dotty. "These days together have made us inseparable friends."

"The Forbes quartette," said Dolly. "Only Bernice is named Forbes, but I mean Uncle Forbes' quartette."

"Yes," said Jefferson Forbes, "my four friends, my Rosebud Garland of Girls."

THE END

THE TOM SWIFT SERIES
By VICTOR APPLETON

12mo. CLOTH.   UNIFORM STYLE OF BINDING.   COLORED WRAPPERS.

These spirited tales convey in a realistic way the wonderful advances in land and sea locomotion. Stories like these are impressed upon the memory and their reading is productive only of good.

TOM SWIFT AND HIS MOTOR CYCLE
Or Fun and Adventure on the Road

TOM SWIFT AND HIS MOTOR BOAT
Or The Rivals of Lake Carlopa

TOM SWIFT AND HIS AIRSHIP
Or The Stirring Cruise of the Red Cloud

TOM SWIFT AND HIS SUBMARINE BOAT
Or Under the Ocean for Sunken Treasure

TOM SWIFT AND HIS ELECTRIC RUNABOUT
Or The Speediest Car on the Road

TOM SWIFT AND HIS WIRELESS MESSAGE
Or The Castaways of Earthquake Island

TOM SWIFT AMONG THE DIAMOND MAKERS
Or The Secret of Phantom Mountain

TOM SWIFT IN THE CAVES OF ICE
Or The Wreck of the Airship

TOM SWIFT AND HIS SKY RACER
Or The Quickest Flight on Record

TOM SWIFT AND HIS ELECTRIC RIFLE
Or Daring Adventures in Elephant Land

TOM SWIFT IN THE CITY OF GOLD
Or Marvellous Adventures Underground

TOM SWIFT AND HIS AIR GLIDER
Or Seeking the Platinum Treasure

TOM SWIFT IN CAPTIVITY
Or A Daring Escape by Airship

TOM SWIFT AND HIS WIZARD CAMERA
Or The Perils of Moving Picture Taking

TOM SWIFT AND HIS GREAT SEARCHLIGHT
Or On the Border for Uncle Sam

TOM SWIFT AND HIS GIANT CANNON
Or The Longest Shots on Record

TOM SWIFT AND HIS PHOTO TELEPHONE
Or The Picture that Saved a Fortune

TOM SWIFT AND HIS AERIAL WARSHIP
Or The Naval Terror of the Seas

TOM SWIFT AND HIS BIG TUNNEL
Or The Hidden City of the Andes

GROSSET & DUNLAP, PUBLISHERS NEW YORK

THE OUTDOOR CHUMS SERIES

By CAPTAIN QUINCY ALLEN

The outdoor chums are four wide-awake lads, sons of wealthy men of a small city located on a lake. The boys love outdoor life, and are greatly interested in hunting, fishing, and picture taking. They have motor cycles, motor boats, canoes, etc., and during their vacations go everywhere and have all sorts of thrilling adventures. The stories give full directions for camping out, how to fish, how to hunt wild animals and prepare the skins for stuffing, how to manage a canoe, how to swim, etc. Full of the spirit of outdoor life.

THE OUTDOOR CHUMS
Or The First Tour of the Rod, Gun and Camera Club.

THE OUTDOOR CHUMS ON THE LAKE
Or Lively Adventures on Wildcat Island.

THE OUTDOOR CHUMS IN THE FOREST
Or Laying the Ghost of Oak Ridge.

THE OUTDOOR CHUMS ON THE GULF
Or Rescuing the Lost Balloonists.

THE OUTDOOR CHUMS AFTER BIG GAME
Or Perilous Adventures in the Wilderness.

THE OUTDOOR CHUMS ON A HOUSEBOAT
Or The Rivals of the Mississippi.

THE OUTDOOR CHUMS IN THE BIG WOODS
Or The Rival Hunters at Lumber Run.

THE OUTDOOR CHUMS AT CABIN POINT
Or The Golden Cup Mystery.

12mo. Averaging 240 pages. Illustrated. Handsomely bound in Cloth.

GROSSET & DUNLAP, PUBLISHERS, NEW YORK

THE GIRLS OF CENTRAL HIGH SERIES

By GERTRUDE W. MORRISON

12mo. BOUND IN CLOTH.   ILLUSTRATED.   UNIFORM STYLE OF BINDING.

Here is a series full of the spirit of high school life of to-day. The girls are real flesh-and-blood characters, and we follow them with interest in school and out. There are many contested matches on track and field, and on the water, as well as doings in the classroom and on the school stage. There is plenty of fun and excitement, all clean, pure and wholesome.

THE GIRLS OF CENTRAL HIGH
Or Rivals for all Honors.
A stirring tale of high school life, full of fun, with a touch of mystery and a strange initiation.

THE GIRLS OF CENTRAL HIGH ON LAKE LUNA
Or The Crew That Won.
Telling of water sports and fun galore, and of fine times in camp.

THE GIRLS OF CENTRAL HIGH AT BASKETBALL
Or The Great Gymnasium Mystery.
Here we have a number of thrilling contests at basketball and in addition, the solving of a mystery which had bothered the high school authorities for a long while.

THE GIRLS OF CENTRAL HIGH ON THE STAGE
Or The Play That Took the Prize.
How the girls went in for theatricals and how one of them wrote a play which afterward was made over for the professional stage and brought in some much-needed money.

THE GIRLS OF CENTRAL HIGH ON TRACK AND FIELD
Or The Girl Champions of the School League
This story takes in high school athletics in their most approved and up-to-date fashion. Full of fun and excitement.

THE GIRLS OF CENTRAL HIGH IN CAMP
Or The Old Professor's Secret.
The girls went camping on Acorn Island and had a delightful time at boating, swimming and picnic parties.

GROSSET & DUNLAP,   PUBLISHERS,   NEW YORK

THE CHILDREN'S CRIMSON SERIES

May be had wherever books are sold.   Ask for **Grosset & Dunlap's** list

The Editors; and What the Children's Crimson Series Offers Your Child

IN THE first place, "The Children's Crimson Series" is designed to please and interest every child, by reason of the sheer fascination of the stories and poems contained therein.

To accomplish such an end, a vast amount of patient labor, a rare judgment, a life-long study of children, and a genuine love for all that is best in literature, are essential factors of success.

Kate Douglas Wiggin (Mrs. Riggs) and Nora Archibald Smith possess these qualities and this experience.   Their efforts, as pioneers of kindergarten work, the love and admiration in which their works are held by all young people, prove them to be in full sympathy with this unique piece of work.

Let all parents, who wish their little ones to have their minds and tastes developed along the right paths, remember that once a child is interested and amused, the rest is comparatively easy.   Stories and poems so admirably selected, cannot then but sow the seeds of a real literary culture, which must be encouraged in childhood if it is ever to exercise a real influence in life.

EDITED BY KATE DOUGLAS WIGGIN AND NORA ARCHIBALD SMITH

THE FAIRY RING: *Fairy Tales for Children 4 to 8*
MAGIC CASEMENTS: *Fairy Tales for Children 6 to 12*
TALES OF LAUGHTER: *Fairy Tales for Growing Boys and Girls*
TALES OF WONDER: *Fairy Tales that Make One Wonder*
PINAFORE PALACE: *Rhymes and Jingles for Tiny Tots*
THE POSY RING: *Verses and Poems that Children Love and Learn*
GOLDEN NUMBERS: *Verses and Poems for Children and Grown-ups*
THE TALKING BEASTS: *Birds and Beasts in Fable*
　　　　　　　　　EDITED BY ASA DON DICKINSON
CHRISTMAS STORIES: *"Read Us a Story About Christmas"*
　　　　　　　　　EDITED BY MARY E. BURT AND W. T. CHAPIN
STORIES AND POEMS FROM KIPLING: *"How the Camel Got His Hump,"*
　　　　　　　　　and other Stories.

GROSSET & DUNLAP, PUBLISHERS, NEW YORK

EVERY BOY'S LIBRARY
BOY SCOUT EDITION SIMILAR TO THIS VOLUME

The Boy Scouts of America in making up this Library, selected only such books as had been proven by a nation-wide canvass to be most universally in demand among the boys themselves. Originally published in more expensive editions only, they are now, under the direction of the Scout's National Council, re-issued at a lower price so that all boys may have the advantage of reading and owning them. It is the only series of books published under the control of this great organization, whose sole object is the welfare and happiness of the boy himself. For the first time in history a *guaranteed* library is available, and at a price so low as to be within the reach of all.

GROSSET & DUNLAP, Publishers, NEW YORK

THE EVERY CHILD SHOULD KNOW SERIES

May be had wherever books are sold.   Ask for Grosset & Dunlap's list

BIRDS EVERY CHILD SHOULD KNOW
By Neltje Blanchan. Illustrated

EARTH AND SKY EVERY CHILD SHOULD KNOW
By Julia Ellen Rogers. Illustrated

ESSAYS EVERY CHILD SHOULD KNOW
Edited by Hamilton W. Mabie

FAIRY TALES EVERY CHILD SHOULD KNOW
Edited by Hamilton W. Mabie

FAMOUS STORIES EVERY CHILD SHOULD KNOW
Edited by Hamilton W. Mabie

FOLK TALES EVERY CHILD SHOULD KNOW
Edited by Hamilton W. Mabie

HEROES EVERY CHILD SHOULD KNOW
Edited by Hamilton W. Mabie

HEROINES EVERY CHILD SHOULD KNOW
Coedited by Hamilton W. Mabie and Kate Stephens

HYMNS EVERY CHILD SHOULD KNOW
Edited by Dolores Bacon

LEGENDS EVERY CHILD SHOULD KNOW
Edited by Hamilton W. Mabie

MYTHS EVERY CHILD SHOULD KNOW
Edited by Hamilton W. Mabie

OPERAS EVERY CHILD SHOULD KNOW
By Dolores Bacon. Illustrated

PICTURES EVERY CHILD SHOULD KNOW
By Dolores Bacon. Illustrated

POEMS EVERY CHILD SHOULD KNOW
Edited by Mary E. Burt

PROSE EVERY CHILD SHOULD KNOW
Edited by Mary E. Burt

SONGS EVERY CHILD SHOULD KNOW
Edited by Dolores Bacon

TREES EVERY CHILD SHOULD KNOW
By Julia Ellen Rogers. Illustrated

WATER WONDERS EVERY CHILD SHOULD KNOW
By Jean M. Thompson. Illustrated

WILD ANIMALS EVERY CHILD SHOULD KNOW
By Julia Ellen Rogers. Illustrated

WILD FLOWERS EVERY CHILD SHOULD KNOW
By Frederic William Stack. Illustrated

GROSSET & DUNLAP, PUBLISHERS, NEW YORK